Death of a Cape Cod Cavalier

M.E. Kemp

L & L Dreamspell
London, Texas

Cover and Interior Design by L & L Dreamspell

ISBN: 978-1-60318-478-6

Library of Congress Control Number: 2012949410

Visit us on the web at www.lldreamspell.com

Published by L & L Dreamspell
Printed in the United States of America

Acknowledgement

For Kay Olan and her magic printer!

For Betty and Miriam

Prelude

Small hands reached out to pull the shiny handle up and free. He swished it around in the salt water to clean the dirt from it. Mama taught him to keep everything clean because that was godly. The little boy wiped it on the reeds that swayed around his feet. What a pretty thing! It shone like an oyster shell with pale pinks and blues and purples as he twisted it one way and another. He took great care of the sharp end because that could cut and hurt him. Mama taught him that, too, when he set the table for the family meal. The little boy looked around. His mother was there on the beach, bent over the sand looking for the tiny bubbles that meant buried clams. They'd have a good dinner today. Mother was such a good cook. Why, she knew how to take an egg, stir it up and cut herbs into it and make it into a feast, never mind her steamed clams and clam cakes. He felt a pang of hunger at the thought of buttery broth mopped up with a chunk of johnnycake. His first inclination was to run to her with his prize—but he knew she would not let him keep it. The knife belonged to someone else—to this man, here, in all likelihood, but the man had no use for it. The boy knew a dead man when he saw one. Drowned, pounded by fists or feet, aged, sick—he'd seen many a dead body. Mama was often called in to help lay them out. There were a great many dead bodies in the Eastham cemetery that Mama helped to lay out.

The little boy shifted his eyes this way and that and stuffed the knife beneath his shirt under the rope that held up his pantaloons. The tide was coming in so he skipped across the beach to the safety of his mother's side.

One

The agitation of the man seemed out of proportion to the letter he waved at us—that is, at Increase Cotton, his cousin, and me, Hetty Henry, cousin to his wife Abigail. Creasy and I had both been summoned to the comfortable home of Cotton Mather, but I might have been a fly on the window for all the attention he paid to me. Even lovely Abigail was ignored by the agitated young minister. She stood behind us, a tray in her shapely hands.

"How can I be expected to just drop everything in Boston and rush off to Billingsgate? I don't even know where the place is! Billingsgate? I thought it was in London. I've a conference of my colleagues in the ministry in five days and I must attend to extend the hand of friendship to our new member. It is essential that I welcome Jacob Joyliffe after all my previous calumnies of the poor man! I shall never be able to forgive myself for my harsh accusations against him. Of course, he was arrested for murder. One cannot ignore such a charge. Still, I should have extended Christian charity. I should have been as objective as you, Cousin, and kept an open mind. Even though Joyliffe was found standing over the dead man..."

Cotton Mather paced back and forth. "And I hardly know this new dead man," he said. "Pierce was a year ahead of me at Harvard College. As you well know, Creasy—oh, and you as well, Hetty—I was a mere lad, much younger than my classmates, but even at that age I possessed a formidable understanding that raised jealousy in the bosoms of certain of my fellow students."

The parchment crackled beneath his fingers. "Pierce was one of the bullies who delighted in tormenting me when I dared rebuke them for their wicked ways. Oh yes, I recall Mr. Pierce and I have long since forgiven him."

Creasy grabbed the parchment from his hand as Cotton Mather strode past us. We walked over to the window and Creasy held it to the light so that I might read it with him. The letter was written in a neat hand with occasional flourishes of certain letters.

Billingsgate, the year 1695

Respected Sir, Mr. Cotton Mather;
It is with sadness that I write to inform you of the
death of Charles Pierce, a former classmate of yours
at Harvard College. The Mather name is known for
its beneficent Urges and you are Requested to address
a grievance that Demands an Expiation. The matter
Requires your immediate presence. My sister and myself
welcome you as an honored guest in our home.
Your Obedient Servant,
Thomas Tiley

Abigail set her tray upon a table. She had brought India tea, a brew her husband hailed for its medicinal value. She stood directly behind me, peering over my shoulder. Dear Abigail was a bit shortsighted. "It's a cipher," she said. She spoke in her usual calm tone.

As soon as she uttered the word the capital letters jumped out at me. "She's right," I said, handing the letter back to Cotton Mather.

"It's excellently phrased," Mather said, examining it with more attention. "An appropriate address—he does honor to the Mather name. Yet I cannot answer the call. People make many demands for my services and I am not able to answer them all. People who know me well do not expect me to pack my trunk and leave my congregation without its guardian upon a whim. My time is not my own, to dispose as I would like." Mather shook his head. His periwig bobbled.

"He's given you good reason," I said. "Look at those capital letters: M-U-R-D-E-R. That's not a whim, Cousin Cotton, it's a cry for help."

"Well, why does this Mister Tiley not come out and say so? Why use a cipher?" Mather's handsome mouth puckered, a sign in him of a stubborn contentiousness only his nearest in kin recognized.

"Perhaps Mr. Tiley is a cautious man," Creasy said, addressing his cousin for the first time. "There may be many prying eyes between here and Billingsgate." He turned to me. "Hetty, where is Billingsgate?"

"It's towards the end of Cape Cod," I said.

"Cape Cod? That den of atheistical pirates?" Cotton Mather waved a well-shaped hand. "I cannot possibly make such a trip."

"I can take you on my ship, if that is what troubles you," I said. "I must go to Billingsgate on a matter of commerce in any event."

Mather graced me with a nod. "I thank you, Cousin Hetty, but I cannot possibly leave my duties here."

"What commerce brings you to the Cape, Hetty?" Creasy turned his lank frame to me.

"Oysters, Creasy, oysters—the best to be had in New England. I have customers eager for them. All I can provide."

"Oh." He handed the letter to his cousin Mather. He moved away from me and wandered to the table where Abigail smiled and poured him a mug of tea. He picked up a handful of nuts and raisins from a bowl.

"You could go in my stead." Mather pointed at his cousin.

Creasy very nearly choked on the raisins.

Mather held up one hand to stop any objections. "I'll see that your congregation of poor widows and rough sailors has the comfort of my sermons, never fear, Cousin. Or perhaps Jacob Joyliffe may be of service to their needs, since he has no pulpit yet. Now that is a good thought of mine. You and Cousin Hetty have had some little successes on these lines—I am the first man to acknowledge your abilities in exposing these malicious perpetrators of murder."

"Yes, and Hetty nearly was drowned the last time, and I was hit on the head. It's not so simple as you think, Cotton." Creasy set down his cup with a determined clank. "And not so safe, either, although Hetty would have you believe it to be a mere stroll upon the commons."

Abigail handed me a mug of hot tea, her brown eyes wide with dismay. Her lips trembled. "Oh Hetty, you did not tell me of the danger! I do not want you to go to this awful place." She turned to her husband, her cheeks flushed. "It's not right of you to ask it of her. Indeed, it is not right. This is man's business, indeed."

I'd never heard sweet Abigail address her beloved husband in such tones of reproach. I was quite moved, as Abigail Mather thought the sun rose and set for the well being of Cotton Mather.

"I'm only going to pick up a cargo of oysters, dearest Abby," I said. I touched her sleeve. "Since I am sailing there, I may as well transport Creasy. He may look into the matter, and if help is needed… Well, I have a captain and first mate and crew to protect us both. You needn't fear for me."

"The…the woman is not being sent by m-me, Abigail!" Cotton Mather stuttered in his frustration. "I would never knowingly send y-your cousin into danger."

"Yes, Abby, listen to your husband." I nodded. "I only offer to transport Creasy in my ship, as I must go there anyhow, on matters of commerce. He will conduct any questioning that needs to be done. I shan't interfere."

Creasy made a choking noise and I gave him a rude glance.

My assurances were met with a sigh of relief. "Yes, Hetty, that is how it should be. Creasy is well trained in the ministry and suited to the task. He will be further protection for you, my dearest cousin. It is man's business, after all." Abigail had the unfortunate habit of parroting her husband's thoughts.

I refrained from snorting. As if I would sit in my little ship's cubby while Creasy had all the adventures. I love my cousin Abigail dearly, but I hadn't enlarged the fortunes of two dead husbands by acting like a little mouse. Meanwhile Creasy stood there smiling at her like a cat with a dish of cream before it. I'd have to keep these two apart. I knew that Creasy admired his cousin's wife more than he should—well, there is much about Abigail to be admired, but not in the way he looked at her. And Abby was so innocent and so sweet to her husband's younger cousin that it only encouraged the young man to act like a lovesick swain. Taking him to Billingsgate would remove him from the temptation to make a fool of himself. Not that I thought Abigail was in the least danger of succumbing to Creasy's charms, however any declarations from him would upset her no end. No doubt she would blame herself for some imagined sinful conduct. Her husband was a master of finding other people's sinful conduct.

Cotton Mather moved with a brisk pace to his desk. "I shall write a letter of introduction for you, Cousin. That will serve, you'll see." He gave Creasy a beatific smile and reached for his quill pen.

I hid my misgivings by lifting my mug of steaming India tea.

Two

A sunny October day made our voyage to the Cape so pleasant that Creasy, who was prone to seasick episodes, stood by the rail for the entire voyage. The *Anhinga* sailed into Billingsgate Bay sleek as the seabird for which she is named. We docked her at Silver Springs, a small settlement with the fortune to sit before huge oyster beds of the finest quality. Fed and nourished by the tides, the oysters grew strong and hardy, keeping well in casks for travel. There was also an abundance of fish; bass, herring and perch, in the bay waters and its streams but they were of no interest to me. Oysters were the gold of Billingsgate. There was a greedy market for these tasty mollusks in Boston Town; a very profitable market indeed. I am not one to ignore a profit.

Creasy's purpose in coming to Billingsgate was to preach to the native peoples, we decided, and to such others as would welcome his sermons.

"That should give you a reason to ask questions, but be careful," I said. "There is need for caution here or the news would not have been sent in cipher." I was not really worried, for Creasy is by nature and training far more cautious of his skin than am I. We were dealing with a murder, however. I talked as we walked up the path to the little hut that served as home for fisherman Thomas Tiley and his widowed sister Margery. I knew them both. It was my guess that the letter with its flourishes had been written by the hand of that quick-witted lady.

Margery Mason greeted us at the kitchen door in an old gray

gown and an apron dusty with flour. The spicy scent of ginger tickled my nostrils and I realized how hungry I was. All my thoughts of oysters sinking down the gullets of Boston merchants and now the smell of baking gingerbread made my innards groan. I knew Margery would relieve my distress. I greeted her with a kiss on the cheek and turned to introduce my companion, whom she greeted with pretty words and dainty hands that left a smudge of white flour upon his coat sleeve.

"Ooo, I'm sorry," she said, dimpling. She had to stand upon tiptoe to rub the spot with a corner of her apron.

My companion gazed down upon her, his long mouth twisting into a grin. "You can make amends by giving me a taste of whatever delight you are baking. The smell is making me drool with hunger."

Margery curtsied low. "You shall have a piece, sir. Let me seat you and I shall strive to relieve your hunger." She waved a hand to indicate we should sit at a wooden table scarred with knife marks. The table was made from an old ship's hatch. Within minutes we were drinking mugs of cider and munching on chunks of dark, spicy cake warm from the oven.

I had misgivings that Creasy did not take his eyes from her. Margery was a little woman with warm brown eyes, thick black lashes and a lively spirit that danced in her eyes. If her nose was a trifle broad for true beauty it was offset by a dimpled chin and a cupid's bow mouth. Creasy was susceptible to fancies for young women; he thought himself quite the gallant.

As we ate she explained that her brother Tom was at work and would not return until dark.

I leaned across the table, placing my hand over hers. I spoke in a low voice, even though there was no one within hearing distance. "Margery, we are here to help you. Creasy, here, has been sent in Mister Mather's place. We have had some success in solving crimes, he and I, and Mister Mather thought we might be able to help. It was you who wrote the letter to Cotton Mather?"

Margery nodded, her thick lashes downcast, hiding her eyes.

"Why the need for secrecy? Why the code?" I asked.

She raised her eyes, then, the brown orbs moist. "We don't know whom to trust anymore. We just do not know. Thomas was one of the two men who dragged the body from the water. Thomas and Abel Cole, who was a good friend of Charlie's. Poor Abel! Poor Charlie!"

I noted her use of the familiar first names. Of course in a small village everyone would know the first name of their neighbor and address him in such an informal manner.

"At first they thought he'd drowned, but as soon as they pulled the body into the boat, they knew." There was a catch in her voice but she continued. "They know the look of a drowned man, you see. Even it's being in a waterlogged state and all swollen, they saw the rent in the coat and the traces of blood on the cloth. Charlie Pierce was murdered! He was stabbed to death!"

Margery's lips screwed downwards and her black brows knit together. I thought she might burst into tears, but she inhaled in two deep breaths and remained in control of herself.

Creasy looked almost as distressed as Margery as moisture filled his own dark eyes. He reached over to pat her arm. "Take a drink of your excellent cider." He waited like an anxious parent until she had swallowed several mouthfuls. "There," he said, "that should help. Did the man—Mr. Pierce—have a quarrel with anyone or any persons in the town?"

"Charlie?" Margery shook her head, sleek dark hair bobbing beneath a linen cap. "Charlie Pierce was liked by everyone. He'd be the first to offer a hand to someone with troubles. Charlie Pierce was a very generous man, and it wasn't just money with him. If you needed an extra hand he'd fish with you. That's the sort of man he was. If you needed new nets...well, Charlie was there with the money, no questions asked." Margery regarded Creasy with mild reproach, her eyes large and soulful as those of a milch cow. "We can think of no reason why anyone should murder him. None."

"Well, we don't know him, you see." Creasy spoke in what

I called his 'comforting the poor female' tone. It was a trick he had, gentling his voice so that it inspired confidences. It worked, too—except on me, of course. "Tell us about him. The slightest thing you remember may well be of help to us," he crooned.

"Well…" Margery paused, folding her hands upon the table. "Charlie came here when he was just a lad. His mother was born here. I think his father had died. I didn't know him then… I was just a baby. His mother was a woman of property, and Charlie inherited. That was about eleven years ago. He has—had—commercial interests in Boston, for he went there several times a year. Oh, they say he is affianced to a woman there. I don't know her name, poor soul. She'll have to be told."

"We shall see to that," I said.

"Who inherits his property?" Creasy kept his voice low but his thin brows drew into a slight frown. "Was he never married?"

Margery shook her head. "No. I'm sure we would have known if he was married."

"You said he was well liked. Did that include women as well as men?" I thought to myself that a personable man is not usually stabbed in the back. And where was the knife?

"Oh, he was a favorite with the ladies. Charlie was always available to act as escort if there was a gathering of sorts. With the men in the village away at sea so much fishing, there were many women—including myself—who asked for his escort. What with the rough sailors in port and the natives and our men gone, it was nice to have the arm of a strong man. Charlie always acted the gentleman—at least in my experience," she said, a bit of color brightening her cheeks. She turned warm brown eyes away from me to Creasy.

"Oh course, of course," Creasy continued his soothing tone. "We must ask questions in order to establish his character, that is all. We must get to know the man—it's the first step before we can begin to find his killer. We have had some successes along these lines, that is why Mister Mather sent us to you." His smile radiated with sympathy for the woman. "Was there a particular woman who called upon his escort more than others, or one who might feel she had a claim to his attentions?"

Margery's brow knit in wrinkles. "Not one that comes to mind." She spoke slowly, adding: "They are all married, except for the two of us widows—me and Annie Wixam, and Annie is in her eightieth year. She's spry and active for her age, but I very much doubt that Annie considers marriage with anyone, much less a man so much younger than her as Charlie Pierce. She's a sharp witted woman, our Annie," Margery added. "It might be worth your while to speak to her."

Margery jumped up from her seat. "I'll get you Charles' clothing. We laid him out here, you see." She left the room for a short period, returning with a string-wrapped parcel that she lay upon the table. "If you don't mind." She backed away. "I'll just go set aside some food for Tom when he comes home." It was evident that she did not wish to see the dead man's clothing.

We heard scraping sounds and pots being set upon the hearth as we unwrapped the package. I unfolded a sheet of stiff paper and lifted a blue coat that was still damp to the touch. The scent of seaweed and mold filled my nose. Creasy reached beneath my hands to lift up a buckram waistcoat and shake it out. Tiny grains of sand sifted onto the table. We held each garment next to the other. The slits in the backs of each lined up together. Both garments were stained with the rust color of blood. We then examined a white shirt, tucked beneath the others. The shirt was slit and stained in the same spot. I felt my anger rise. Stabbed in the back! What a cowardly assailant—or assailants, as the case may be. A man who stabbed in the back was a cowardly cur, the lowliest of the low. Justice must be done this poor man. I knew that Creasy, standing by my side with eyes of coal and grim lips, felt the same compulsion.

Of course, that is why we'd come to the Cape—for justice. Our forefathers may have had their faults but their strength was a commitment to justice for great and small, for rich and poor alike under the law. Holding the clothing of the dead man in our hands made it much more of a personal quest.

"We'll find him. We'll find the man who did this." I turned to address Margery.

Margery, bent over the hearth, straightened as I spoke. She nodded, down-turned lashes covering eyes that were usually merry. After a moment she joined us.

We decided that she and I would question her neighbors. Gossip in a small settlement like Billingsgate was its entertainment. Creasy would approach the men, but not until he had established himself as a minister to the local native, the Punonakanit. That was our ostensible reason for coming to Billingsgate: he to preach and me to visit my friends Thomas and Margery.

"Are they very fierce?" Creasy asked, blinking at Margery.

"Not at all. They live much the same way we do, by fishing you know. They have lived here forever."

Creasy turned to me. "Are you sure you don't want me to come with you? I would be some protection for you both." He glanced at Margery. "I shouldn't want you to walk into any danger. This is a murderer we're looking for, after all."

"I cannot think my neighbors would harm me, sir," Margery said, laying a hand upon his sleeve to placate him. "With the two of us in broad daylight I can ease your worry about that."

"I can take care of myself," I said, my tone less than warm.

"Oh, I have no fear for your safety, Hetty." Creasy waved the long fingers of his left hand in the air. His other palm was busy covering Margery's small hand. "Hetty will take good care of you." He smiled down at her.

I'd have to remind him that we came to Billingsgate for a purpose and it was not to ogle a small woman with sympathetic brown eyes. I wondered if the serpent Jealousy was responsible for the death of Charles Pierce. Was one of the husbands jealous of the attention Pierce gave to his wife? Was it one of the ladies themselves? Might one woman be jealous of his attentions to another? I hoped to pick up a little gossip on those lines. Was there really a fiancée in Boston or was that a way for Pierce to keep the ladies at bay? Well, a few discreet inquiries would solve that problem. If there was a lady waiting for him in Boston then I had the duty to inform her of his death. Or maybe I'd send Creasy on that sad task. He was good with wilting females, even if his syrupy sayings drove me to distraction. Yet I had to admit that the grieving widow in torn sackcloth perked up like a chickadee when the young minister Increase Cotton set out to soothe her grief.

Too bad he hadn't been around when either of my two late husbands died. Although I probably would have thrown him bodily out of the house if he had come at me with those puppy eyes and plaintive platitudes. Ah well, we all meet grief in our own way.

Three

Tom Tiley walked with Creasy to the small fishing settlement of the native peoples, the Punonakanit. There, Tiley introduced him to Samuel Glossip, a native preacher of the people. It was under Glossip's willing auspices that Creasy met the male members of the Punonakanit. Giggles that came from behind the bark walls of the round meetinghouse informed him that the women were watching him as well. He was asked to preach a few words once he'd been shown to his hut and unpacked his bag. To this request he was well pleased, glad to find such a pious peoples, anxious to hear the words of the gospel.

Tiley and Glossip accompanied him to a square hut built much like those of the settlers of Silver Creek. Inside he found a table, two stools, a bed with a coverlet in bright colors, a large chest by the bed, and a line of pots and pans next to the hearth. Leaning over the hearth was a young native woman. She stirred a large kettle from which issued tantalizing smells.

"Judith!" Glossip spoke in a commanding tone.

The native woman turned and straightened, wiping her hands upon her apron. Beneath the apron she wore a simple gown of gray linen.

"Judith, this is Mister Cotton." Glossip turned to Creasy. "Mister Cotton, this is Judith Littlefeather. She will cook and clean for you. Judith will see to your needs."

The native woman, a plump little soul with merry black eyes, made a deep curtsy.

"Well it certainly smells most appetizing, Miss Littlefeather." Creasy, ever the gentleman, bowed to the lady.

"Oh, call her Judith." Glossip waved a brown hand. "Everyone does."

"Call me Creasy," Creasy said, grinning. "Everyone does."

The native woman ignored his jest. "I am making a cod stew, with johnnycake to go with it." She gestured with a large spoon. "Would you gentlemen care to share it with Mister Cotton? There is more than enough to go around."

Tom Tiley shook his head in slow regret. "I have to return. My sister expects me."

Glossip shook his shining black head as well. "I'll come back for you, sir, after you've eaten," he addressed Creasy.

The two men took their leave and Creasy busied himself with emptying his bag, which did not take long as it consisted of several shirts, a brown silk waistcoat, a pair of breeches and a black, threadbare cassock with several clean bands. As soon as he stood up Judith beckoned him to the table. She served him a bowl of stew, fragrant with herbs. She set a round pan of cornbread and cut several golden slices for him.

"This is very good," he said.

She looked at him. "You need fattening up."

"I have no doubt I'll be as stout as a hog if I eat like this for very long." He picked up his spoon and applied himself to his stew. A piece of johnnycake served to wipe up the dregs.

"How long do you remain with us?" Judith took up his empty bowl and spoon. "I'll clean up," she said when he offered to help. "You go give your sermon."

Creasy stood up. "I don't know how long I will remain here but I hope it's for a few weeks, if I am fed as well as this every day." He wiped his long mouth with a piece of linen.

Judith gave a small curtsy and went about her business.

How nice to have someone to cook and to clean up for him, he thought. What a luxury! He rarely cooked his own meals, favoring a local tavern or the contributions of the ladies of his congregation who took pity upon his single state, but he felt it his duty to keep the minister's house, which belonged to the congregation, in good order so he swept and dusted himself.

A knock upon the door brought the broad face of Samuel Glossip come to escort him. Creasy shrugged himself into his black coat, straightened the white fall at his throat and met the gentleman at the door. For his text he had chosen one he thought would appeal to his native listeners; Isaiah 9:5: *For every battle of the warrior is with confused noise; and garments rolled in blood.* Even the peaceable Punonakanit seemed to enjoy his text, upon which he expounded for the greater part of an hour. A short talk, but he felt it to be very effective. It was much applauded and acclaimed, at any rate.

Darkness had fallen by the time he returned to his little house. A lit candle upon a stand by the door and the banked fire in the hearth gave him enough light to see. He undressed, put on his nightshirt and fell upon the bed with a sigh of relief. A successful sermon always left him with a comforting feeling of exhaustion. He burrowed his head into the pillow and closed his eyes.

In a state between waking and sleeping he nevertheless caught the creak of a floorboard. Creasy rose upon one elbow, calling out, "Who's there?"

Before he could move the covers of the bed were raised and a plump body fell over his. Two chubby arms were thrown about his neck and a soft body pressed against him. If this were murder then death must be an angel of the Lord, he thought, his senses overcome for a moment.

Creasy sat up, removing the arms from around his neck. "What are you doing?"

"I am here to serve your needs." Two hands pulled at his nightshirt.

"What? What?" Creasy shook his head. Perhaps this was a dream, after all.

"It's the way of my people. I am here to serve your needs."

Creasy scrambled to the end of the bed. “Really, Judith!” He evaded the stretching arms.

“It is our way. I shouldn’t do it if I didn’t like you. That is my choice.” She held out her arms to him.

“No, Judith. No! It’s not my people’s way.” He dodged the outstretched arms. His throat felt dry.

“Do you not like me? Shall I find someone else for you?” She spoke in simple enquiry.

“I like you very well, but…” Creasy’s protest came out in a croak.

“Do you not have the needs of a man?”

“Of course I have the needs of a man.” Creasy felt quite indignant.

“Oh, I thought because you are a famous preacher that you may not have those needs.” She offered the words as an apology.

“Well, I do have those needs. But it is our custom to court a maid and then to marry.”

“Oh, I am too young to marry but I am allowed to lay with a man.”

Creasy grabbed at the coverlet, pulling it up to his chin. “Go home before your mother and father discover you are gone.”

“They know I am here.” She leaned back against the pillow, placing her hands behind her head. Her breasts were like two melons. “It is an honor to be chosen to serve you. There are many young women of my people who are jealous of me. But I am the best cook among them, and so I was chosen.” She spoke in a complacent voice, recognizing her own worth.

“You are a good cook, Miss Judith, and that is how I prefer you. Please get dressed and go home. I shall see you at breakfast.” Fully clothed, he hoped, keeping the thought to himself. Creasy turned his face resolutely to the wall, waiting until she had dressed herself. He got up and escorted her to the door. Seeing her safely out he dropped the bolt on the inside of the door, making certain it was secure.

Judith Littlefeather explained to her parents that the English minister stayed celibate, as had their warrior ancestors who remained so to retain their prowess in war. The minister would lose his powerful preaching ability should he succumb to the temptations of the flesh. Her mother and father nodded in respect.

Four

Margery and I made our first stop at Charlie Pierce's house, which was little more than a plain box with sturdy furniture inside it and the smell of tobacco still in the air. The walls were whitewashed and the floors were of pine boards. Only the bed with its four posts and bright yellow comforter made the house a little richer than would be thought. A quick search revealed nothing that would serve as a motive for murder. I checked the desk for letters but no telltale missives of love were there. In fact, I could find no personal correspondence of any sort, just some bills and receipts. It was frustrating, as a desk will usually reveal a great deal about its owner. There were no clues as to a fiancée in Boston or any other favored ladies. I began to suspect that Pierce had made up an imaginary fiancée to keep himself safe from importunate females. Nor did Margery find any missives or any tokens of affection in the great chest at the foot of the bed, just a dozen white shirts, white stockings, smallclothes of black, two waistcoats of superior cut, a bottle green coat and various bed linens.

Mr. Charles Pierce remained a cipher, much like the one Margery had sent to Cotton Mather. Yet there had to be a reason for his death. It was up to me and to Creasy, with Margery and Tom's help, to uncover that reason. Sometimes reasons were difficult to uncover, but we were used to that, Creasy and I.

Our next stop was to the wife of the second man who'd helped to pull Charlie Pierce's body from the water. Margery thought Mrs. Abitha Cole might know something about Pierce.

Mrs. Cole was a thin woman with weak blue eyes and a spotted apron, lank strands of blonde hair peeping from a plain cap, As soon as I noted the apron I mentally scolded myself for my lack of charity. Our visit was unexpected and the woman was poor, by the looks of the one room house. The whitewash on the walls had turned dingy with age and the wooden stools looked rickety. The bed in the corner was hidden by the dark interior, with only one window on the far side of the kitchen to let in light.

I turned my attention to the little boy who peered at me from behind his mother's petticoats. Creasy made friends easily with children. I did not have his easy manner. Unless the young ones were exceptionally bright and spirited, I did not as a general rule take to them, nor they to me.

This boy was about five years of age and shy, by the looks of him—his thin face was a younger image of his pale mother. I pulled a coin from my pocket and held it out. "A coin for your boy, Mrs. Cole? Will he take it from my hand?"

The woman reached behind her, pulled the boy to the front and gave him a push towards me. The poor lad looked quite as pale as if he had seen a ghost, but he grabbed the coin in a grimy paw and retreated behind his mother's skirts.

"Nay, he needn't be frightened of me, Mrs. Cole, I shan't eat him." I forced a smile.

I was glad when Margery interrupted us. "Mrs. Cole's husband helped pull Charles Pierce from the bay. Where exactly was that, Mrs. Cole?"

"My husband and your brother found him," Mrs. Cole said. "He must have told you it was off the Meadow on Billingsgate beach. I was there earlier in the day, but I did not see the body. I was digging for clams. Mr. Cole thought the man had drowned until they took him into the boat, then they saw the slit in the coat."

I noticed streaks of grey in the blond strands of hair that hung about her face. Life was hard and these people had little, I thought. Mister Pierce lending them money—might there be some resentment there? People sometimes grew to hate those from whom they were forced to borrow, no matter the good intentions of the lender. This I knew from experience. I needed to know more about the man.

"Mrs. Cole, please forgive me if my questions seem impertinent, but I was told that Mr. Pierce used to escort the wives to functions when the husbands were at sea..." I left the question unspoken.

The woman nodded. "There was no scandal about it," she said. "The men were content to let Charles—Mr. Pierce—take their wives to Eastham or Chequesset Neck to visit friends or relations or to frolics like strawberry parties. Our men can ill afford to lose a day's work for such frivolities. Oh, if there was a sickness in the family, of course that is not a frivolity. And Charles was of such an accommodating nature he was always ready to oblige. One always feels safer in the company of a man."

Safe from whom, I wondered. "Do you have problems with your natives?" I asked. Here I'd gone and sent Creasy to the native village. Perhaps I'd placed him in danger!

"No," she said, shaking her head. "Not with the Indians. They give us no trouble as we hardly see them. They keep to their village. No, there are rough sailors who drink and curse and gamble down by the wharf. They profane the Sabbath and may even accost a poor woman if she is without a gentleman's escort." She wrinkled her narrow nose in disdain. "A woman just feels safer with a man about."

I thought of a certain unscrupulous pirate on the Island of Manhattan and agreed with her. I made a point of surrounding myself with strong men whenever I had to deal with Alphonse Delahousie. Had I not done so, I might well end up on a slave ship in the Mediterranean. For all the frills and frippery with which he adorned his person, my friend Alphonse was as deadly as a viper. Business interests dictated that I deal with the man, and I knew he liked me in his way, but trust him with my life, I did not dare.

"Was there any talk of Mr. Pierce and one of the ladies he

escorted in particular?" I asked. "Did he favor one woman over the others?"

Mrs. Cole's pale eyes widened. "But Charles Pierce was affianced to a lady in Boston. We all knew that. We are most of us married." She glanced at Margery and lowered her eyes, as if in modesty.

"Thank you, Mrs. Cole," I said, stifling my urge to snort. As if married ladies never flirted nor mislaid their vows. I knew a blacksmith's wife who bragged… Well, never mind. I rose to my feet. "You've been very helpful."

Less helpful was Mistress Bethesda Mayo, who did not even invite us inside. "I know nothing of his death," she said in a wooden tone, speaking from the doorway. "I cannot be of use to you."

She shut the door in our faces. Behind the door it sounded as if a pack of wolves were inside chasing a deer. Benches overturned, howls filled the air and pottery smashed. I looked at Margery with brows raised in unspoken question.

"Children," she said with a perfunctory frown. "She has seven of them. All boys."

I had noted that behind her back Mistress Mayo concealed a stick.

Five

Our next visit was to a man with whom I had a slight acquaintance. Robert Roach was a rotund little man with graying ginger-colored hair and whiskers and bushy graying brows over sharp blue eyes. Roach was pleasant enough but his wife, Madame Roach, was thin, dark and exceedingly loud of voice. The couple had one daughter, Lucy, upon whom they doted. Lucy was a plump young woman of eighteen years with blonde flowing curls and eyes of cornflower blue. Men were tongue-tied in her presence—my sailors being no exception. They would stand like statues, caps doffed, all eyes fixed upon the young lady as if she were an Admiral of the Fleet. I tried to conduct my business with Mister Roach at his own place of commerce.

Roach supplied the local fishermen with ropes, tar, netting, hooks and other necessities of the trade. He also ran the nearest thing to a tavern in the shed behind his house. While his was also a one-room house it was larger than the other homes in Billingsgate with a loft bedroom where I guessed Lucy must sleep. I caught a glimpse of carpet at the head of the ladder and a fold of flowered curtain. The stools by the hearth were upholstered and the cooking vessels gleamed on hooks above the fireplace. There was a wooden cupboard in the kitchen corner.

Madame Roach set a tray of dry cakes and watered ale before us. Margery stiffened in a noticeable manner as Madame poured out the ale. I knew it was watered as soon as I tasted it. Perhaps Roach had pecuniary troubles. Keeping that daughter in ribbons and lace must cost him many a penny. That young woman was shooed out of the room as soon as I ventured to speak of Charles Pierce. Lucy turned to protest her dismissal but her mother's wiry but strong arm pushed her out of the room and closed the door. Madame Roach placed a finger to her mouth in caution and continued to lean against the door, listening for the retreating steps of her daughter. Satisfied, she turned to us.

"Lucy is such a sensitive young woman—we do our best to keep her from unpleasant news, you know." Madame Roach's lowered voice could have wakened the dead.

"She is our only child." Master Roach gave a smug look at the door through his shaggy brows.

I noted Margery's wooden expression as I set down my mug. "Yes, we've come about the death of Charles Pierce." I paused. "That must certainly be unpleasant news. I've been sent by Mister Cotton Mather of Boston to find out about his demise." The mention of Cotton Mather's name impressed Madame. She raised thin brows as she seated herself upon a bench beside her husband.

"If I may ask some questions..."

Robert Roach nodded, leaning forward with one hand upon his knee. He had a trick of looking up at one through graying eyelashes.

I addressed his wife. "It's well known that women accepted his escort when convenient. I can understand that, as your husbands are often away for days at a time."

"Oh, but my husband is never away like that." Madame interrupted in a braying voice. "He may travel to Boston for supplies as you well know, Mrs. Henry, but he is only gone for the day, rarely overnight. I never had the need to call upon Mr. Pierce for his escort. Never."

"Your daughter, perhaps?" I smiled winningly. "Young people will enjoy their frolics."

"We should never allow Lucy to step out with a single gentleman," Madame sniffed in audible displeasure.

"We would not." Robert Roach spoke in a firm tone. "Charlie

Pierce is—was—too old to be of interest to my daughter in any event. No doubt she regarded him as much a graybeard as her father." His mouth parted in a smile, displaying uneven brown teeth.

"Is there a woman he was seen to escort more than others?" I asked, addressing Madame. I judged her sharp eyes would notice more than her husband where other women were concerned.

Madame shook her head. "If you had asked me this question beforehand I might perhaps have had an answer for you, but this moment I can't think of any woman he favored, if that's what you mean."

Robert Roach rose to his feet. He was a short man yet he held himself with upright dignity. "What do you insinuate with your questions? Poor Charlie Pierce drowned. Isn't that enough?"

"Charlie Pierce was dead before he was drowned." These were the first words Margery had uttered since she'd introduced me to the Roaches. Her voice was hard.

"Why—what can you mean?" Madame called out. Dark eyes nearly popped from her thin face.

I wasted no words. "Mr. Pierce was murdered. He was killed before he went into the water." Sometimes blunt speaking is more effective than shilly-shallying around a topic.

"Wh-why, that is terrible!" Madame stammered. Her pale skin turned white, like blue-tinged milk beneath the cream.

Robert Roach's eyes narrowed beneath his shaggy brows. "We have not heard this. We know nothing of this. How was he killed? Do they know who did it?"

"The Cape constable is away in Barnstable," I said. "There has been no attempt to find the killer. That is why Mister Increase Cotton and I have been sent by Mister Cotton Mather of Boston." The announcement had the desired effect, at least upon the lady, who clasped her thin hands and uttered a cry of admiration.

"His many public and ministerial duties keep Mister Mather in Boston. Mister Increase Cotton, as you may know, is cousin to Mister Mather. He is elsewhere right now on ministerial duties, but no doubt he will want to question you for himself. We have had some successes in uncovering villains, Mister Cotton and I." This was not a boast on my part. Creasy and I had uncovered several killers in recent years. Creasy was good at ferreting out guilty secrets and I had the means to accumulate information.

"B-but…everyone liked poor Charlie!" Madame shook her head in disbelief.

I judged her reaction, almost shouted, to be sincere. "That's why we are asking about his escorts, whether there might have been a jealous husband, or perhaps a jealous woman?"

"A woman?" Roach frowned. "Surely not a woman. Why, a woman would not have the strength to drown a man. But you say he wasn't drowned. Well, then, how did he die?"

"Stabbed, sir. He was stabbed in the back."

"Ah." Roach thought for a moment. "Do you have the weapon?"

"No. We don't have the weapon as yet." I did not like to admit this. Where was the weapon? What kind of knife was used? Everyone had knives: kitchen knives, fishing knives to gut and hack, whittling knives… How on earth were we to know what kind of knife was used or where to find it? "What we need to know is why someone would want to kill the man. It seems that everyone liked him!"

"We did! We all liked him! Poor Charlie." Madame gave a loud sigh.

I thought her truly shaken by the news. "Please think about it. Perhaps there was a jealous husband? A jealous woman?" I asked, my eyes upon the woman.

Madame's eyes were red-rimmed. "We wouldn't know—but you might talk to our neighbors, the Warrens. They're on the other side of the inlet. They'll know if anyone does. They seem to know everything that goes on in Silver Springs, and they'll tell you about it, too. Talk, talk, talk—it's most unseemly to gossip as they do." She rubbed her hands as if they were cold.

The woman clearly did not approve of her neighbors but the Warrens sounded like a good omen to me. We hadn't seemed to learn a thing so far. If Charles Pierce was so well liked, then who killed him? I wished I knew. Even gossip might help to provide some sort of motive for the murder of such a popular person.

As we left the house we were accosted by a whisper from the bushes. "Hsssst!" Margery and I stopped and looked at each other. A snake? But it was too cold for the sluggish reptiles. The hedge before us rustled, and a woman's form wrapped in a blue cloak, face concealed by the hood, pushed aside the dry branches.

"Were you talking about Charlie?" The woman's voice was young and high-pitched.

"Lucy?" Margery stepped forward, peering at the woman.

"Shush!" Lucy raised a plump finger to her bow-shaped lips. "My parents mustn't know I'm speaking to you."

Margery lowered her tone to a conspiratorial whisper. "What do you want?"

"Were you talking about Charlie Pierce?" She repeated her question.

"Yes, we were. Do you know anything about his death…who might have killed him?"

"Is it true he was murdered?" The young woman's whisper sounded urgent.

"Yes, it's true. Do you know who might have killed him?" Margery repeated the question with more emphasis.

"Well my father might have, if he found out I was seeing Charlie…as a friend," she added with haste. "Charlie is—was—older than I, but he was someone to speak to…to tell one's troubles, you know. I only kissed him a few times. My father thinks I'm a child—he'd keep me locked in my room if he could." Resentment was clear in her voice and in the knitted blonde brows. "Charlie escorted most of the wives—why shouldn't he take me to a corn-husking? And if he wanted a kiss as payment, what's that to me?" The young lady shrugged beneath her cloak. "He didn't deserve to die for it, did he?"

"Are you sure it was only a kiss?" I asked, curiosity getting the best of me.

"Oh yes," the young lady said. "Charlie was too much the gentleman to take advantage of a young lady's innocence."

I'm sure Margery looked as skeptical as I and the young woman pouted with her pretty lips. "That's what he told me," she said. "Those were his very words, even though I encouraged him, well…to take a few liberties. I am tired of all those boys who hang about me like bees. They are quick enough to take liberties. Anyway, I have to go. My father will be looking for me." With those words the young lady disappeared, shrinking back into the bushes.

Margery and I just looked at one another. "Would you believe a daughter accusing her father of murder just because he keeps her under his eye?" Margery shook her head in wonder.

"Tries to keep her under his eye," I amended. "He isn't as successful as he believes. Anyway, Master Roach must be considered as a suspect. His wife, as well, though she seemed truly shocked at the news. We must keep an open mind. Remember that, Margery," I said. "An open mind is essential to an investigation of this kind."

"But what reason would Ellen Roach have to kill Charlie if he never escorted her?" Margery asked.

"That is what we must find out for ourselves. There could be any number of reasons. Perhaps she found out about those stolen kisses of Lucy's or perhaps she was jealous of her daughter. We have to consider all these things. No one is above suspicion."

We turned and resumed our walk. My thoughts tumbled around in my brain like the arms of a windmill. Everyone we'd spoken to had nothing but praise for the generous man. So far only Mistress Bethesda Mayo had refused to speak to us, but I was rather glad of it for I could not see myself trying to hear her words with seven brats fighting each other over our heads. We'd have to speak to her husband some time, perhaps out of doors. Perhaps we could catch him when his fishing boat docked. I had hoped that the wives would speak more freely before Margery and me as fellow females, and perhaps most of them would. We'd only just begun our questioning, after all. I took some comfort in that.

Six

I spoke my bewilderment to Margery as we walked around a marshy bend to the next box of a house. "If Charlie Pierce was so liked by everyone, who killed him? That is what I don't understand." She did not answer me, her brown eyes lowered to the ground. "With most murders there is some kind of reason for it. Jealousy, greed, some quality in the victim that irritates others," I went on. "Some reason why you'd murder a man. I don't see that here."

Seagulls flapped overhead, squawking and squabbling like ministers over a point of doctrine. They wheeled and dipped in the crisp blue of the sky. Human voices were also raised inside the humble hut we faced. I noted that a shutter hung askew. When Margery knocked upon the door the voices stopped shouting. We shifted our feet for several moments before the door opened a crack.

"Yes…who is it?" A man's head peeked out, brown hair sticking up in spear points, chin bristling with black stubble.

"It's Margery Mason, Tom Tiley's sister. I've brought a friend. May we speak to you and to Mary?"

I noted a round face like an overgrown elf peeping behind the man's back.

"Oh, neighbor Margery. Well, come in!" The man spoke in forced joviality, opening the door wide enough so that we could enter. "Everyone's welcome in my home."

We squeezed through the door as the man did not move aside. Margery handed him a sack, which she'd kept beneath her cloak and I heard the clank of glass upon glass. The sack disappeared from sight.

The little house was neat and clean with a biblical painting in dark shades upon the wall. We sat upon a crude but sturdy bench before the hearth. Margery made me known as her friend, Mrs. Henry of Boston. "Jack. Mary, we'd like to ask a few questions concerning the death—"

Jack Warren interrupted, waving a square-shaped hand in our direction. "Charlie Pierce." He turned his head. "I told you so, Mary. I said someone would be around asking questions. He never drowned, that Charlie. I told you there was something more to it." He turned back to us. "Terrible thing. Did you see him, Margery? Did you see his poor body? Charlie Pierce was a good swimmer. Me, I can't swim. Mary can't swim, either."

"We laid him out. He didn't drown." Margery's voice was crisp. "Charlie died by other means. It was murder. Can you think of anyone who might have had a reason to kill him?"

"Oh, there were one or two in debt to him. He wasn't as well liked as he thought he was." Warren spoke in a casual tone. The man looked down at the ground, fingering a leather thong around his neck. "I could name names if I wanted."

"My husband is a smart man." Mary nodded her head, strands of thick brown hair swaying around fat cheeks and a pointed chin.

"I suggest you name names," Margery said, addressing the husband. "Mrs. Henry has authority from Boston to look into this matter." She motioned with one finger at me, as if to indicate that I was a magistrate. Well, I wasn't but my second husband, Mr. Henry, had been. I'd learned from him that justice was a matter for the community and that it applied to the poor as to the rich.

I frown and puckered up my mouth to look stern.

"I don't want to get anyone into trouble." The man raised square, hairy hands in the air as if to protest.

"We shall be discreet," I said. "Your name need not come into my report." Well, I would report back to Cousin Cotton Mather, at least that much was so.

"Well, then, I suppose it is my duty..." He leaned forward to address us. "I heard that Daniel Freeman and Eldad Mayo owed Pierce quite large amounts of money. They took out loans for boat repairs and my aunt Philomena—you know, she lives out on Chequessett—she heard Freeman curse out Pierce one day when she was visiting her friend Miz Hornby with a receipt for the chilblains. Well, the weather was comin' on to cold and Miz Hornby suffers from them greatly, you know, on account of when she—"

"Get on with it," Margery said, interrupting the narration.

"Daniel Freeman has a real temper, my aunt says. Then there's Fishy Mayo. He don't like nobody and he was mad as a hornet 'cause Charlie took his wife to the harvest dinner. Well, Fishy was out for a couple days and didn't come back in time for the dinner like he promised. He said as Miz Mayo should've just stayed at home with the little ones—she has five of 'em—but her sister come over from Truro to help out, so Miz Mayo went with Charlie. He didn't sit with her or nothin' though, and nobody had any bad thoughts about it except Fishy."

"You didn't take me to the harvest dinner and I wanted to go." Mary cuffed her husband upon the shoulder with a closed fist.

"Now Mary, you know I hurt my back and couldn't help out with the harvest this year. The dinner is for those who work at the harvest. We'll go next year, if the good Lord be willing." Warren rubbed his shoulder as he spoke.

"We know it was common for Mister Pierce to escort women on these occasions," I said, hoping to avoid a marital spat. I turned to the wife. "Did he ever escort you, Mrs. Warren?"

Mary Warren shrank against her husband. "Oh, no."

"I take my Mary any place she wants to go." Warren spoke with assurance.

"You didn't take me to the harvest dinner." Mary clutched at her husband's sleeve, twisting it into a knot.

"Now, now...we go to plenty of places, Mary." Warren patted his wife's hand. "I take you out to pickin' strawberries and we go blueberrying with everyone else and the clambakes—"

"Did Charlie Pierce attend these events?" I asked.

"Most times," Warren said.

"Did he escort one woman more than any others?" I asked, persisting.

Jack Warren shook his shaggy head. "Not that I saw. Charlie liked all the ladies equal." He grinned, adding, "And he warn't always the gentleman with them, either, though the ladies won't tell you that."

"Mrs. Warren?" I turned to that lady, thinking she might have noticed more than her husband, as women will.

The woman only shook her head, shrinking further behind her husband. I wondered if she were not quite simple in her mind.

Margery thanked the couple for their time and we took our leave.

As we walked I turned to my companion. "You don't seem to care much for the Warrens."

Margery sighed. "I should be more charitable, I know, but Jack Warren has never done a day's work in his life. That bad back…well he's had it as long as I've known him. He lets Mary clean the house, fish in the bay, collect mussels and oysters and beg from the neighbors if necessary. Then he makes lists for the improvement of her character! I'd like to take his lists and shove them up his arse, that's what I would like to do."

I giggled. "You took them some food, I noticed."

"I take them some preserves and butter for he'd never think of providing them for Mary. Come winter they pretty much live on the charity of their neighbors, and the neighbors are poor enough themselves. Hetty, I'd best be quiet now."

I honored her wish while we followed a small stream to the next house. This house looked even more weathered and in need of repair than the Warren home, but there was a cheery patch of orange and red-leaved bushes next to the door and a few pink roses bloomed on a vine that crept up the side of a sunny wall.

"This is Annie Wixam's. She's a friend of Charlie's and she's eighty years old, so I don't think we can consider her for the murder." Margery spoke in a quick whisper, "She's sharp as a nail, though, and may be able to help us find the killer. Nothing gets past Annie."

I looked forward to meeting the redoubtable lady. She lived up to my expectations, as an iron-haired lady opened the door to greet us before Margery had even knocked. Annie Wixam was stout-figured and hardy with a weathered face and hands like hams. I would never have guessed her age, for she looked capable of navigating at the helm of a schooner through a hurricane wind.

"Come in, come in!" She beckoned with a large hand.

"This is Mrs. Henry from Boston." Margery introduced me without preamble.

"Ayuh. Come to find out who stuck a knife in Charlie's back."

Word certainly spread fast in this tiny spot, thought I, but it was only to be expected. I looked around the room. The dark interior walls were lined with fishing nets and lines; pots and buckets stood in a row on the dirt floor.

Annie led us to a table of silvered wood and we sat upon a bench while she poured two large mugs of cider. In less than a moment I drank mine down in rapid swallows as I discovered I was thirsty from the walk and from talking to what seemed to me reluctant strangers. The liquid had a slightly sour taste that was interesting and not unattractive. I set the empty mug upon the table before me.

Margery sipped at her cider while Annie Wixam nodded at me in approval. Would that I had been more careful of my swallows, for I soon felt a buzzing in my ears and Mistress Wixam appeared to have grown an extra head. I stared at her with amazed eyeballs.

Margery nudged me in the side. I made an effort to recall my wits and my eyesight. I caught the words: shark and ducks.

"It swum up the creek here after my ducks, it did, but it got stuck between the banks and couldn't turn around so I took my pitchfork and killed it, I did." Annie gave a satisfied nod. "Ain't no shark going to eat my ducks. I feed 'em all winter long, you know."

"Annie, you should have called Tom."

Margery's objections were met with a shrug of a hefty shoulder beneath a worn smock. "Just a fish," she said. "Now, do ya' know who stabbed poor Charlie in the back? I'll take my pitchfork to him, too. Coward."

"We were hoping you would have some idea," I said. "We are asking everybody if Charlie Pierce had any enemies, or any reason to do him in. He seems to have been a friend to everybody here."

"Charlie was a good man. Can't think of anyone here who would do him a harm. He allus' stopped to see if I had my provisions. Tried to get me to move in with my sister in Providence but I ain't about to leave my ducks."

"We heard that a man named Mayo owed him money," I said.

Annie only snorted. "Fishy Mayo wouldn't stab a man in the back. 'Sides, he was over to Provincetown when it happened. Musta' been plenty people who seen him there." She paused for a moment, eyeing me. "Who tol' you it was Fishy?"

I shook my head, unwilling to reveal my source.

"Must a' been that mealy-mouth Jack Warren." Annie gave a snort. "If he warn't such a skinny-shanks lazy good-for-nothin', I'd think he done it, but he's too lazy and scared a pup to stab a man in the back. Only with his tongue, that one."

I kept my lips sealed and Margery looked grim. "Did you see Charlie on the day he died?" she asked.

A shake of the iron-gray head was our answer.

We took our leave then, me noting with some admiration the pitchfork hanging upon the wall next to the door.

As we returned to the Tiley home the germ of an idea formed in my still somewhat cider-fogged brain. I suggested that we regroup at night to discuss what we'd learned, what we hadn't learned and what we could do to provoke more information.

SEVEN

I sat by the hearth and watched Margery throw chunks of salted pork into the great iron kettle hanging above the fire. The sizzle and the smell teased my hunger, distracting me from my whirling thoughts. Margery poured a pitcher of milk into the kettle and a cloud of steam rose. With quick hands she threw in a bowl of potato chunks and then a platter of fish strips. In a matter of minutes she had set upon the table four large bowls and four spoons. As I noted the extra spoon, Tom Tiley entered the kitchen door with a friend of his in tow, a young man with bold dark eyes, a square jaw and straight black hair pulled back and held by a black ribbon.

"Hetty, this is Cody." Tom introduced the young man as he slumped onto the bench at the kitchen table.

The young man nodded to me but his eyes were on Margery, who had turned back to the hearth and the great kettle and was busy ladling the fish stew into bowls. She placed the bowls before each of us, filling her bowl last and taking her seat on the bench by me, across from the two men. She bent her head and seemed intent upon eating her chowder, ignoring the smile that hovered on the lips of the young man named Cody. The creamy white chowder reminded me of something: the image of me all in white, dressed as a ghost.

I raised my head, the spoon halfway to my mouth. "You know..." I paused, taking care with my words. "Margery and I spoke to quite a few people today and I have the idea that somebody knows more than they are saying to us. We may be able to trick them into confessing—at least into telling us what they are hiding."

Margery raised her head and Cody literally growled at me. "When I catch the bastard that did it I'll beat him until he wishes he were dead as Charlie." The man's black eyes glinted like hot coals.

"I take it you were a friend of Mister Pierce," I said.

"None better," he growled.

"I played this trick once before and it got results," I continued with my story. "The men we tried it on did confess." Unfortunately, they didn't confess to the murder we were investigating at the time, but to little indiscretions. That information I kept to myself. "And nobody knows what Creasy…that is, Mister Cotton, looks like because he is away preaching to the natives. And we've got Mister Pierce's clothes." I went on to explain what I had in mind.

Cody hooted in obvious approval. Tom Tiley looked thoughtful. Margery's brown eyes shone, but she remained silent.

"Would he ride by on horseback?" Tiley asked.

"No. No horses," Cody said. "Horses can be traced and they leave little piles of shit. Nothing scary about that."

"It seems to me that the Warrens would be quick to spread the word they'd seen the ghost of Charles Pierce, so they should be the first ones to see it. He struck me as a gossip. Am I correct in that assumption?"

All nodded in unison, heads bobbing like ducks on a windy pond.

"What if they are sleeping? You can't do it in daylight." Margery was a practical woman.

"I'll see that they wake up, don't worry about that." Cody grinned like a wolf.

The man's teeth were white and straight, unusual for a New England man. I thought to myself that I might have to keep an eye on Mister Cody and his enthusiasm. "Anyway," I continued, relating my plan, "it all hinges on Mister Cotton. He must agree to play the role. You two men would be recognized. I think Pierce's clothing will fit him nicely. I'll send him a note in the morning, and we'll meet here again, tomorrow night after supper. Is this agreed?"

The two men nodded.

I was forced to wheedle a bit that afternoon but Creasy finally agreed to take part in my scheme. Although he'd not participated in my former ghostly deception, he knew of it after the fact. All he'd have to do, I promised, was to put on Charlie Pierce's clothing and walk past a window. I repeated that promise to him in the evening. We were all gathered around the table in Tom Tiley's home.

"How will they see me in the dark?" Creasy was nothing if not practical.

Rather to my surprise Cody volunteered an answer. "I can rig up a small lantern with tin cones that will reflect the light up and down. You can tie it around your leg and it will outline you—at least from a distance. Should be a ghostly effect."

I nodded my approval.

"Can I try it on before I do all this parading about? And just where am I to parade?"

I could tell he was still wary of my scheme.

"Oh, I'll have it ready by tomorrow night." Cody Jewett gave a confident nod.

Tom Tiley grinned. "He's good at inventing things, Cody is. It will work, and the fellow you're going to fool is a half-wit. Warren will tell the whole Cape what he saw. The murderer is sure to hear about it."

"You'll try it out at Jack Warren's house, then?"

The two men nodded.

Margery made a muffled sound. "But you might scare Mary, and that wouldn't be right."

Tom turned to his sister. "It'll take more than a ghost to scare Mary Warren—she's as tough as old leather. And she'll talk, too, and she goes more places than Warren does."

He turned back to Creasy. "You'll just walk past his window. We'll make a noise or something to bring Jack to look out, then you'll walk past. It'll work, sure enough, and the whole town will know he's seen the ghost of Charlie Pierce. Then we'll have you walk along the shore a day or two later. People will be looking to see you by then. We ought to be able to scare Charlie's killer out."

"What if he's scared out with a sword in his hand?" Creasy asked, his voice close to a squeak. "What if he attacks me?"

"Then you'll run." Cody grinned, showing his even teeth.

"We'll be right there," Tom said, his voice firm. "You don't have to worry, we'll keep a sharp eye on you."

"I'm sure this will frighten the murderer into confessing," I said, speaking in my most reassuring tone. I was pleased that Tiley proved to be a willing conspirator and his friend Cody even more willing to play a prank.

"It would frighten me." Margery shuddered. "I don't think I want to see this. I don't have to go with you, do I?"

Cody stepped behind her chair, placing his hand on the newel knob. "You don't have to do anything you'd rather not do." He smiled down at her, touching her brown hair with a light finger.

Margery lowered her head, hiding her face from him. I wondered what lay between the two of them. Cody was obviously fond of her, but how did Margery feel about him? She'd not given any open indication to me that she cared for him, yet one had to admit he was a handsome brute if you liked that bold sort. I did, as a rule.

"Oh, Hetty!" Margery lifted her head and turned to me. "Will you go with them?"

"I wouldn't miss it for the world," I said.

"Oh, please be careful, Hetty. All of you." She clasped her hands as if to pray for us.

Perhaps we would need her prayers, I thought, but my mouth curved into a smile at the promise of the mischief we were about to attempt.

We agreed to gather late the next evening, when Cody would bring his lighting invention.

I spent the rest of the next day preparing for the big event, drying and brushing the articles of Charlie Pierce's clothing that Creasy would wear. We gathered after a dinner of oyster chowder when a brief knock upon the door brought our inventor. We looked up in expectation. Jewett presented to us a small tin lantern with holes in the sides to reflect light. "I can't get it to reflect much below the waist—if I had more time I might be able to extend it out—"

"Let's see how it works." I waved my hand at his modest disclaimer.

Cody beckoned to Creasy, who stood still while the inventor tied the device about Creasy's leg. Cody lit a candle stub inside the device.

We all trooped outside to witness the effect in the dusk. With the lantern outlining his movements, Creasy strode across the broken shells and tufts of beach grass on the lawn. It was true we couldn't see much of his legs; Creasy appeared to float in the air with an even more ghostly appearance than we anticipated.

Margery clapped her hands. "Cody, you are clever!"

"I'd be frightened out of my wits!" Tom Tiley gasped, but as he was bent over holding his sides with laughter, his declaration did not impress the company.

"It works!" I called out to reassure our walking experiment.

Creasy turned. "Ouch! The thing's getting hot!" He twisted his body to blow out the candle but could not reach the lantern.

I ran over to help, blowing out the stub in one breath. "You won't have to wear it for long, Creasy. Just to walk a few steps and we'll be there to help you take it off." As I spoke I untied the leather strip that held the lantern in place. Cody bent beside me and took it from my hands.

"Maybe I can find a way to extend the thing out from his body."

"It will do as is. You won't have to wear it long," I repeated. "Now all you have to do is put on Charlie Pierce's clothing. As it's almost dark, you might as well put them on now." I gave him a push in the direction of the little house. Creasy had been unusually stubborn lately, refusing to get into the spirit of the thing.

Margery, standing in the doorway, grabbed his hand and led him inside. She made soothing sounds of encouragement, telling him how well he'd done.

We stood around, silent, until Creasy opened the door and stepped out. The moon shone down upon him in a long blue coat with elegant lines. He looked like another man.

Cody cradled the tin lantern in his capable hands as we walked the short distance to the humble hut of Jack Warren. Creasy's brows knit as he questioned Tom Tiley.

"Where are we going? What am I supposed to do? Where will it be done?"

"I'll show you a spot on top of a sand dune," Tiley said in a calming voice. "All you have to do is to walk across it and step down the side into the beach grass. We'll be there waiting for you."

"Don't worry," I said. "I'll blow out the candle as quick as can be. The tin won't even get hot."

Creasy continued his grousing. "Why me?" He had asked me the same question twice before in the afternoon.

"Because you fit the clothing," I said, remaining patient with the man. If I were in his place I would be so excited and eager the other two men would have had to hold me back. Some people have no sense of adventure, I reflected. Not that Creasy wasn't brave, or that he couldn't hold his own in a fight, I will say that for him. It must be his Harvard training that makes him so cautious. His cousin Cotton Mather is even more of a mouse when it comes to a harmless prank. Oh, I will say this for both ministers—when a principle is involved they stand strong. Both had opposed the tyranny of Royal Governor Edmund Andros. They could have been charged with treason for their opposition, but they both signed the declaration stating their reasons for arresting the Royal Governor and sending him in chains back to England. Charges of graft and corruption in the New England colonies held little interest to Crown officials, however, and Edmund Andros received a slight slap on the wrist and a governorship in another colony. So goes it when the site of government is so far removed from the governed—

My thoughts were interrupted and brought back to the matter at hand.

"I'm too tall to wear Charlie's clothing," Tom Tiley said, "and Cody is too broad."

"Hey! I'm not fat!" Cody made an immediate objection.

"I never said you were fat. Just broad in the shoulders, I meant. You'd rip open the seams of the coat and you could never button that waistcoat, either. You're not fat, Cody, but you are broad in build." Tiley threw a comradely arm over Cody's shoulder and turned to address Creasy Cotton. "You are near to Charlie's shape as may be, Sir. It's in a good cause," he said to reassure the skeptical expression upon my friend's face. "And you may well flush out an assassin. Charlie Pierce was a good man. He shall not die without justice for our loss."

"Justice must be served, by whatever means," I said, reminding Creasy of his duty.

"Yes, but you must admit this is a strange way you've devised, Hetty. Leave it to you."

I ignored his grousing and his bitter words.

Cody grinned at me. "I think it's a fine plan. Jack Warren will spread the word that he's seen Charlie's ghost, he'll spread it far and wide. If the killer doesn't confess right off, someone's sure to know something, and sure to tell us."

Tiley cautioned us to be quiet from this point on, leading us down the dunes until he came to a sand bank where we could hide and observe the dilapidated home of Jack Warren. There we crouched while Cody set about tying the small lantern's leather strap around Creasy's stockinged ankle.

"Stand up," Cody gave the order with a hiss.

Creasy obeyed and Tom Tiley struck a spark from his tinder box and lit the stub of a candle which he held for a moment before setting it gently into the lantern. The effect was truly unearthly. I had to stop myself from clapping.

"There's no light in Warren's house," Creasy said, peering into the night. "Perhaps he's gone to bed. How is he to see me if he is asleep?"

Cody rose with caution and peered in the same direction. He nodded in the dark. The moon was covered by cloud but we could see his head bob. "I'll sneak over beneath the window and bang on it. That's bound to get him up, and when I hear him moving I'll wave my arms and drop to the ground. That's your signal to start walking. Don't worry, I won't be seen. I'll get away."

Cody bent at the waist and scuttled like a giant crab across the sand to the Warren hovel. From where we hid we heard a loud bang. Within a minute a pale light and a white face appeared at the window.

"Walk!" I shoved Creasy in the back and he stumbled forward.

In the dim light of the lantern Creasy seemed to float across the sand. The effect was just what we'd hoped to achieve, and I was so taken up with our success I did not see what happened at the house. I became aware of chuckles and heard the churning of feet running across the sand, but at that point I was too busy kneeling at Creasy's ankle and blowing out the lantern. Creasy was cursing with impatience that the thing was too hot and would I hurry and untie the strap, which I did. The contraption fell to the ground. We forgot about it at Cody's whoops of laughter; all of us stood to receive him.

"What happened?" We spoke as a chorus.

"He fainted! Did you see him? He dropped like a stone." Cody gasped for breath.

"What happened? I couldn't see!" Creasy said, frowning. "I was too busy walking with that damn...awful contraption burning my leg."

"It worked, Creasy! It worked! You looked just like a ghost. Why, I almost thought you were the spirit of Charlie Pierce!" I clapped him on the shoulder. "It couldn't have gone better."

"Jack took one look and fainted dead away. I saw him drop.

His eyes went back in his head and he dropped like a stone." Cody's own eyes sparkled black as burning coals.

"What about his wife? Did we frighten her, too?" I asked, feeling a sudden prink of conscience. I hadn't thought about poor Mary, but I certainly hadn't meant for her to suffer.

Besides which I knew how upset Margery would be if the woman were frightened out of what little wit she had.

Cody shrugged a shoulder. "I didn't see her. Maybe she's still sleeping."

"Mary's tough—don't worry about her. We'd better get out of here." Tom Tiley grabbed Creasy's arm and propelled him across the sand.

We followed the two men, Cody still chuckling under his breath.

Tiley turned back to inform us he would escort Creasy to the native town and return with Pierce's clothing. I could hear Creasy talking with excitement but could not make out his words. I think he had enjoyed himself in spite of his misgivings.

Cody and I turned off on a different path back to the house. I accepted his arm, but when that arm laced around my shoulder and a hand slipped inside my smock to cup my bosom I slapped the hand away.

"For shame, sir! I thought your affections were engaged by Tom's sister," I said.

Cody's bold eyes glinted with the look of a wolf sighting its prey. "I will wed Mistress Margery, but just this moment I am with a woman who excites me beyond my imagination. Hetty Henry, I've never met a girl with your mind for a prank. Don't you think we should celebrate our success tonight?" His arm slid back around my shoulder, drawing me in against his body.

I've always liked a man with a strong arm and a bold eye but just now my thoughts were of gray eyes, an aristocratic nose and a long, sweet mouth. Alexandre Bernon is a Huguenot refugee living in Boston. "No." I pulled away.

He regained my arm, tucking it under his, and we walked on while he regaled me with the delights to be found in his bed and all the treats of passion I should enjoy there. I did not think to listen but one or two must have found their way into my ears. I recall something about a rope and a headboard… His lips whispered words of intrigue, "I want to lie with you here, now—right here upon the sand. You'd like it, Hetty, I swear you would. I'd make you faint from my thrusts, I know it. I'm as big as a man could be."

Cody was very persuasive, but the thought of my Huguenot's sparkling gray eyes kept me steady. I broke away from him and ran forward to the home of the woman to whom he was engaged. I burst through the door as if Lucifer was at my heels. Perhaps he was.

I told the tale of our prank. Cody kept silent, smiling when I came to the part about Jack Warren fainting in fright.

"I hope he didn't hurt himself when he fell," Margery said. "I hope Mary was not too frightened. We mustn't punish poor Mary for Jack's flaws."

Cody, who sat beside her, reached out a square-shaped paw and rested it upon her shoulder. "I think Mary was asleep. I didn't see her or hear her move about." He reached over, choosing a pumpkin muffin and munched upon it. Margery had provided a basket of the treats and set out small plates waiting for our return.

I picked up my glass of cider and sipped, hoping to hide from Margery my disgust with the man. How could he be so devious, making up to one woman when he'd just been seducing another? I would not disillusion my friend, however much it might be my duty. Who knew but that once the man was married with little ones to feed, he'd be too busy to employ those wandering hands upon another woman. Fishing was a hard life. If they married I would pray for Cody's fidelity. Upon reflection and examination of my own conscience, I had to admit that I might have succumbed to the man's honeyed words had it not been for the existence of Alexandre Bernon, my handsome refugee. I have room in my thoughts for only one man at a time. I have always been thus.

Eight

The next morning Margery and I received an early visit from an excited Jack Warren, who barely remembered to doff his knit cap before greeting us.

"I've seen the ghost of Charlie Pierce! Oh…excuse me, ladies. I don't want to frighten you but he walks abroad! He does! I saw him with my own eyes, and a fearful sight it was! I recognized him by his clothing, for he wore that blue coat, the one they found him in. I told Tom and Cody about it. I spied them as they went off to their boat and I ran out to see them. That Cody, he's one who likes his joke but he had no jokes for me this morning. I told him I see the ghost walk on the dunes. It was just past dusk, it was, and I see the ghost clear from my window—the moon, you know. There was a full moon last night, so I could see plain as day. I tell you, ladies, it was a scareful sight and only the protection of the Lord kept me safe. My prayers kept the ghost from accosting me, I tell you, I went down on my knees and begged the Lord to keep me safe from Charlie's spirit, and the Lord heard my prayers!" Warren drew a breath.

"Where did it go?" I took the opportunity to slip in a question.

Warren waved his cap with vehemence. "It disappeared, it did. It just disappeared. It had a glow about it and it just disappeared! I tell you ladies, I was never so scared in my life. The hairs stood up on my head, I know they did. I got right down on my knees and prayed for my life, I can tell you!"

It was Margery's turn to interrupt. "And Mary? What about Mary? Was she very frightened?"

Warren shook a shaggy head, his hair sticking up like the bristles of a porcupine. "That's another reason I had to thank the Lord, and I did, I did thank Him." He fingered a red bruise above a sandy brow. "We had a fight yesterday and Mary took the boat across the bay to stay with her mother. Now that was a blessing, that quarrel, because she was spared a dreadful sight! Oh, the ways of the Lord are beyond our knowing, all praise to Him." Warren clasped his hands together. He lifted his head for a brief glance into the Heavens. "Wait until she hears what I saw! I'm on my way to her mother's house right now, I only stopped by to warn you about the ghost—and I stopped by Annie Wixam's, too, and I'd best warn Mister Roach and his wife. They wouldn't want their Lucy to see such a sight and I hope I may spare them in the telling."

"I hope Mistress Wixam wasn't frightened by your tale," I said. That old woman wasn't frightened of any living creature, I knew, but even her pitchfork couldn't stop a ghost. I hadn't thought of that when we'd planned this prank.

"No, no. She only said as she's seen stranger sights." Warren twisted his cap in his hands. "She's an old lady but she's strong. She give me some bread and cheese for breakfast. I was that excited I rushed out without eating anything! Now, I don't mean to frighten you ladies, but you'd best stay in at night and shutter your windows good. That's what I plan to do. Now I'm off to fetch my Mary home. I thought I'd better warn my neighbors, as is my Christian duty."

"That's good of you, Jack. Wait a moment and I'll send some pumpkin bread back with you. Do you have milk?" She bustled about as she spoke.

"Yes, ma'am, we have milk that Misses Mayo give us from her cow." He accepted a package, nodded to me and thrust his cap back upon his head. Margery accompanied him to the door.

Margery sat back down at the table while I chose another pumpkin muffin. "I hope no one gets hurts by this trickery," she said. "Did you see the bruise over his eye?" She seemed to accuse me with her tone.

"He said he quarreled with his wife. Besides," I answered, "he fell backwards when he fell to the floor, Cody said he did. Do they often fight, Warren and his wife?"

Margery sighed. "It's unfortunate but it's so. Mary has a temper—she's been seen to hit him and even to pound upon him. Jack tries to defend himself but sometimes he strikes back. The men intervene if they see it, but..." Her voice dropped.

"I think I'd pound his head if I had to live with him," I said.

Margery giggled.

"And he'd be thrown out on his arse to earn his bread," I added. "Bad back...I'd give him a bad back. A few whacks with a broom, that's what he'd get from me, the lout. I'd suspect him of murdering poor Pierce except that I can tell he's too lazy and weak-willed to do such a thing. Am I right?" I all but accosted poor Margery in my indignation. She merely nodded, suppressing a smile as her dark eyes sparkled.

We followed in Jack Warren's wake, Margery and I, our steps not nearly as urgent as that aggravating busybody. One belated realization hindered our thoughts, and it came to both of us at once.

"What do we do if someone does confess to us?" Margery turned to me as if I knew the answer. "I wish we'd brought Tom with us. We are only two women."

Why hadn't we waited? That was an excellent question. I could have sent a note to Creasy asking him to accompany us. I could have taken a sailor from the *Anhinga* but the ship had sailed with its succulent cargo. I suppose we were both too anxious to wait. It took a moment for me to think of an answer.

"We'll keep him in confinement at Mister Roach's home until such time as the constable arrives." I thought that would suffice, as Roach had an outbuilding for storage. I was certain he kept the door locked lest some poor beggar take off with a piece of fishing line or a fishhook. I tried to think charitable thoughts of the man, as was my duty, but there was something about him I did not trust.

"What if it is Robert Roach who confesses to the murder?"

Margery had a very practical way of looking at a problem. I

had an answer ready for that, as well. "We'll insist that he keep to his house until the men return from fishing. We'll stay there with him." I was not afraid of the little man. We were the same height; he was in poor physical shape with a potbelly, while I knew I was strong and hearty in health. I could handle the tiller in the middle of an ocean squall, just as well as Annie Wixam.

Seagulls squawked over our heads as they circled in the air above us, hoping for a bit of bread or a crumb of food. They soon flew off in the direction of the wharf where the fishing boats docked. The boats were out at sea now but there might be a scrap of bait left behind or the guts of a fish splattered over the old wooden boards. Seagulls are birds of the most optimistic nature.

Our first attempt at a confession came at the home of Mistress Abitha Cole. Her little boy spotted us as we approached the humble hut. He ran into the house with a shriek. Mistress Cole was quick to answer our knock.

"We seem to have frightened your little boy," I said. "I'm sorry for it."

Mistress Cole ushered us into the kitchen and settled us on a bench by the hearth fire. The logs crackled with blue and orange flame, giving out a comforting warmth. The day was bright and sunny but the morning air was chilled. I looked at my surroundings, noting the number of worn skillets, trivets and pots set in the corner and a great kettle hanging from the lug pole. Strips of pumpkin and strings of apples were hanging from the clavel pole before the hearth. The strings added a spicy scent to the air. It was a neat and cheerful scene.

"Did Jack Warren visit you?" Margery asked with an abruptness that seemed to me out of her character.

Abitha Cole seated herself upon a stool before us, her knobby fingers twisting together in agitation. "Oh, I can't tell you how glad I am to see you both! Jack's news has me in such a fright! I am so glad for your company—we women must cleave together lest the spirit come to haunt us! I doubt that Charlie's ghost would bother the three of us, do you? Oh, I am sore afraid of ghosts and

Jack Warren saw it last night. How brave of him to fight it off! I declare I would have fainted dead away had I seen it!" The woman dabbed at her eyes with a piece of cloth she held in her worn hands. "And no husband to protect me."

Margery leaned forward, placing her small hand on Abitha's arm. "Calm yourself, Mistress. I'm sure if your conscience is clear you need fear no visitation from the dead."

"Yes," I said, tamping down my eagerness. "Is there aught that you should relate to us? We women must keep together, as you say. Speaking to us may ease your conscience." I did not expect this poor woman to have murdered the man, but she might know who had.

"Oh dear, oh dear!' Abitha covered her eyes with her cloth and burst into sobs. In a muffled tone she made her confession. "I'm afraid I let poor Charlie steal a kiss or two last month when he escorted me home from a husking party." She gulped. "Oh, I knew I shouldn't have let him take such liberties, but I'd had a glass or two of punch, and the moon was full and big and orange over our heads… Oh, and I carried a rose pomander that smelled so sweet! And there was Charlie, quoting from the Songs of Solomon. Lord forgive my sins!" She stopped, raising a thin, tragic face to us.

The thought of this faded woman as an enchantress made me think that Mister Pierce must have had a few too many glasses of punch himself. I restrained my urge to snicker. Just in time my better self intervened to suggest that perhaps it was true gallantry on the gentleman's part. Perhaps the lady needed some attention to make her feel worthwhile? I'd no lack of attention from the male sex, ever. Well, being a widow of wealth helped, but there were many women who received nothing but neglect from their menfolk. I'd observed this over the years. Who was I to begrudge another woman her memories?

"Oh, I don't think you'll be bothered by the apparition," I said. "After all, Mister Pierce must have liked you very much. I think the apparition is out to avenge his murder, that's why he has come back. The only one who need fear him is his murderer."

Margery sprang up, placing an arm around Abitha Cole's shoulder. "You needn't worry we shall tell a soul what you have told us, Abitha. I agree with Hetty—Mistress Henry—you need not fear a visitation. Relieve yourself of any such thoughts. I'm glad we've had this talk."

We took our leave and walked on in silence except for a brief comment from Margery. "Poor woman!"

I nodded, my thoughts on the Song of Solomon and the possible downfalls the verses had brought to many a poor maiden. *Behold thou art fair, my love; behold thou art fair; thou hast dove's eyes*; and *Thy cheeks are comely with rows of jewels, thy neck with chains of gold.* What woman could resist such poetry? Charlie Pierce was something of a devil with the ladies, I concluded.

We followed a crushed-shell path to the door of the next cottage, that of Fishy Mayo and his wife. We were fortunate to find both husband and wife at home, Fishy having suffered a complaint of the bowels during the night. Did the man suffer from a complaint of the conscience, I wondered?

Margery introduced me to the nods of the couple, word having spread of my arrival as soon as I'd set foot over Margery's doorstep. Margery commenced to ask if they'd heard the news from Jack Warren. She did not have to complete her question before the couple answered with energetic nods. Margery continued gamely on.

"We are two poor females with no protection, what with Tom out fishing. We seek your company in case the spirit of Charlie Pierce comes before us! Oh, it is so frightening!" She copied the wringing of hands of Abitha Cole, a nice touch.

"No need to be afraid, ladies." Fishy Mayo rose with some difficulty from a cushioned bench. "Here, have a seat if you please." He waved his hand to the bench and we seated ourselves. I looked around, noting a clean if sparsely furnished house with benches by the hearth and a large table, unpolished but sturdy, with two more benches for seating. Pots, poles, tongs and other instruments for cooking stood in neat array next to the hearth. Mayo himself had a plain but pleasant face and a friendly demeanor.

"No need to be afraid," he repeated. "Charlie Pierce was as good a man as ever lived. If indeed it is true and his spirit walks, it must be because he seeks justice for his murder. Women and children need have nothing to fear from him."

Fishy's wife, who resembled Abitha Cole to a great extent except for a softer profile and a shy smile, grabbed a stool and placed it so that her husband could seat himself before us.

"There are those of us who will see to it Charlie gets his justice on this earth," Fishy said, his mouth tightened into a thin line. "There's not a man of us who's not indebted to him in some way. I don't mean in money terms. It's more than that. We'll pay that debt by finding his killer. Daniel Freeman's eldest we sent to Barnstable to fetch the constable, but we shan't wait on him." Fishy turned to standing wife. "Martha, get the ladies a cup of our new-pressed cider."

I drew back a trifle, the memory of Annie Wixam's potent brew still in my mind. Margery's clear countenance reassured me somewhat, and I accepted a cup of the sparkling amber drink. The fragrance of fresh-crushed apple filled my nostrils as I bent my head to drink and my tongue was rewarded with sweet fresh orchard flavor. I realized I was thirsty and downed my cup of juice in one continuous swallow. Before I could even compliment my hostess she replenished my cup from a white pitcher she held with both hands. I glanced down into the depths of dark liquid amber and drank without apprehension.

"There's nothing so good as the first pressing," I said to Mistress Mayo's nod. She seemed pleased with this small compliment.

"Join us for dinner," Fishy urged.

His wife seconded this notion with an eager smile and a shy gesture toward the hearth fire. "We've a nice boiled eel and we've pumpkin sauce and samp. There is plenty," Martha Mayo said.

I placed my hand over my middle. "Margery fed me so much

at breakfast I'm as stuffed as a pigeon. I thank you for the invitation. It's most kind of you!" I meant it. Under other circumstances I would not hesitate to accept, but we were on a mission here and we'd other people to see.

Next we knocked upon the door of Robert Roach. The door opened with such alacrity that Margery almost fell into the room. Madame Roach, whose given name proved to be Ellen, nearly dragged us bodily inside. Two spots of red brightened her white cheeks and her mud-colored eyes shone bright as those of a lizard.

"Have you heard?" She pushed us toward two straight-backed chairs across a small table from a stiff-backed couch. Ellen Roach seated herself upon the edge of the couch, jiggling her thin body up and down in her excitement. "The ghost of Charlie Pierce walks abroad at night! I knew it! I knew there was more to his death than an accident! Oh, my husband insists that he fell upon his knife or that one of his fellow fishermen mishandled his knife in an inebriated state and is afraid to admit it. A drunken brawl... that's how Charlie died, he says, but his ghost coming back to haunt us tells us a very different story. I knew it. I said all along that the man was murdered. His ghost would not walk unless it sought vengeance for murder. Everyone knows that." She fell back against the couch, a gleam in her beady eyes.

Margery settled her skirts and tucked her petticoats primly around her legs before she looked up and addressed Madame. "But who would murder Charlie? We all liked him. He never did anyone any harm."

I watched Madame's face. The glittering black eyes and the quivering of the narrow lips reminded me of a rat smelling out a tasty bit of cheese. She leaned forward in her eagerness to address us.

"Oh, you all think him such a fine fellow..." She dropped her voice. "He lent his money out freely enough, and now that he is dead that money will not have to be paid back, will it? Only think of that. I dare say most of the men in Billingsgate were in debt to him. I'm sure they have thought of it, and one of them acted upon it."

She clasped her hands together as if her claim could not be argued.

I jumped at the harsh tone Margery used in answer. "Which man would do such a thing? Name a name, if you dare."

"You think I won't?" Ellen Roach tittered, her eyes sharp as a rodent. "That Fishy Mayo, for one, and his friend Daniel Freeman for another. Oh, there are plenty of others, including your friend Cody Jewett. You can check my husband's records for the names. Just see who bought new nets and lines and hooks and all." All of a sudden she held her finger to her lips, gesturing for our silence. We heard the soft click of heels on the wooden floor and her daughter entered the room.

Lucy's blonde curls peeped from a lace cap that I would have envied did I not own a similar lace cap, and mine with a rosette on the side. Still, the lace was pretty.

Ellen raised her voice. "Well, ladies, my husband is not at home for the moment. I can't say when he will return." The woman rose to dismiss us, her mouth twisted in a little smirk.

Lucy Roach greeted us with a pretty curtsey. "Mrs. Mason and Mrs. Henry, how nice to meet you again. Please do not leave on my account. Mother, may we not offer the ladies a cup of that new India tea that Father has just received?"

Ellen Roach's dagger look at her daughter should have sheared off that young woman's blond lashes. The older woman turned to us with a grudging offer of tea, but we declined in unison.

Lucy held out her plump hands. "Let me at least show you ladies to the gate," she said, her smile like a ray of sunshine. She swept before us before her mother could speak. At the gate she stopped, pretending to have trouble with the latch. Her blonde curls hid her lowered face.

"My father stayed with friends in Roxbury on the night of the murder," she whispered. "I wrote to the daughter who confirms that he was there for the day and spent the night. He did not return before Charlie was found. A great weight has been lifted from my shoulders. I know you will understand." She unlocked the gate and stood there, waving a farewell as we walked down the path.

"That must eliminate Mister Roach," I said, adding, "if she was not telling a lie. Perhaps she feels guilty for suggesting him to us before. She might be protecting him." I had wished that it might be the little man with the red beard and the sharp eyes of a fox and could barely keep my voice from echoing my thoughts. "Now whom do we see? What other suspects have we?"

Margery plodded on, her head down in thought. I could barely hear her words when she spoke. "I don't believe Lucy would kill anyone, do you?"

That she even suspected Lucy took me by surprise. "I don't think she would get her pretty dress dirty, and there must have been some blood involved, so no. I don't think she killed Charlie Pierce. We should keep an open mind, though." As soon as the words were out I chastised myself for my own suspicions. I went on. "There's her mother, Madame Roach. I'll wager she knew more about those stolen kisses between her daughter and Pierce than she'll admit. It's easier to pull the wool over a father's head than a mother." I spoke from experience here.

"Ellen didn't seem to feel guilty to me." Margery raised her head, gazing at me for confirmation. "She's a small woman. I think it must have taken some strength to stab Charlie and then to throw his body in the bay. I can't imagine Ellen Roach doing it, that's all. I can't imagine any woman doing it."

"Oh, she probably has the strength to stab him, and she could have had help moving his body. She doesn't have the height, that's what bothers me," I said. "From the tear in his coat I think the killer had to be taller than Madame Roach, unless she stood upon a stool."

Margery shot me a skeptical look from beneath a fringe of black lashes.

I wanted to change the subject but all I could think of was

Cody's bold manners, but I didn't think Cody was a very wise subject. I'm well aware that men have different notions of being faithful before marriage, but I wasn't about to inform poor Margery that her intended had roving hands and nasty thoughts.

"Who else shall we see?" I asked, instead.

"There's the Freemans. No doubt Daniel is out on his boat. Perhaps we should wait until tonight to speak to them. We can take Tom with us then. Daniel has something of a temper, although he's always been a good friend to us. Oh, this is so hard for me!" Tears welled in her eyes.

I waited while she gained control of her emotions. The crunch of crushed shells beneath our feet and the cheerful calls of birds filled the silence that fell between the two of us. Beach grasses waved upon the mounds of sand and the blue waters of the bay sparkled in the distance. Clumps of brush red with rose hips and scarlet leaves formed an untidy border on both sides of the path we walked. This was a simpler life, I thought, longing for a cup of rose hip tea. Yet the remembrance of bustling streets, of handsome buildings, of stylish men and women, of convivial dinners in taverns and private homes with luxurious interiors, of busy wharves filled with ships tall with masts and riggings, convinced me I could no more leave Boston than a babe its mother's arms.

"I've known these people all my life, you see, and now I'm trying to get one of them to confess to murder." Margery dashed away at the tears in her eyes using a clenched fist.

"Justice," I said. "Justice for Charlie Pierce. That's why you wrote to Cotton Mather. That's why Creasy and I are here. The man or woman of the least means deserves justice equal to the richest. That's what my late husband, the magistrate, taught me."

"Yes." Margery spoke in a tired voice. "Justice for poor Charlie."

We both lapsed into silence for the short remainder of our walk.

Nine

Shortly after the prank with the lantern, the trick that Creasy still deplored, Judith Littlefeather came to prepare Creasy's breakfast, as usual. Lately Creasy had taken to eating his other meals at Tom Tiley's home in company with Tiley's lively sister Margery, Hetty, Tiley and his friend Cody. The only time he saw the native woman was at breakfast, although she continued to keep his hut neat and tidy. Creasy felt a slight unease in her company, although Judith seemed perfectly unconscious of her attempt at seduction. Certainly she had not attempted to repeat it.

This morning she fed him a beefsteak with a tasty corn dish rather like an unsweetened corn pudding, which meal he swallowed in unalloyed enjoyment. The prank of posing as a ghost seemed to have given him a strong appetite, much as he regretted his role in that prank. Judith set down a fresh mug of cider for him to drink. She stood by his side for a moment, eyeing him.

From the bosom of her blouse she took out a small leather bag with a long string of hide. She flung the strap over his head. "Here. Wear this at all times. It will keep you safe."

Creasy fingered the little sack of leather. "Keep me safe?" He raised thin black brows. "Why, what's in it? Why must I wear it? Safe from what?"

Judith placed a plump hand over his. Her eyes, usually gleaming with good humor, were overcast and shadowed by thick black lashes. "There are bad spirits abroad. Wear it and it will protect you."

Creasy gave a laugh tinged with a note of bitterness. "If you mean the spirit of poor Charlie Pierce, I can assure you that spirit will do me no harm. I have banished that spirit forever." If Hetty Henry thought he would repeat that silly stunt and walk dressed in the dead man's clothing, she was much mistaken. Mistress Hetty had her own way once too often; she'd had her way too much, for too long, and had grown accustomed to ordering others about.

Creasy lifted the leather bag, looking at it with curiosity. "What's in this?" As he squeezed it the faint scent of dried grass teased his nostrils.

"Herbs," Judith said. "It will protect you."

Judith looked so unusually solemn that Creasy felt he should placate her. Perhaps he should scold her for pagan superstitions but he did not have the heart. He'd all ready rejected the poor girl once. What harm could herbs do? Herbs were good gifts given by the Lord to benefit all mankind. Even their scent was of medicinal value in some cases.

"Yes," he said. "I will wear it." Why argue with the woman? Her people had proven to be pious and good, enthusiastic about his words. Surely he could grant the native woman this one little favor.

Judith nodded, satisfied. She went about her work, saying no more to him.

Creasy left to make several visits among the Punonakanit. First was to an old woman to whom he brought the comfort of the Christian religion. His second visit was to a young man whose sickness came out of a bottle of rum. Perhaps he could frighten the young man by telling him he'd drunk poison, for rum certainly acted as poison to the native constitution.

These duties accomplished, he sauntered away from the native village, taking the path that led to Silver Springs. Perhaps he would be in time to take dinner with Margery Mason, the woman with the sweet brown eyes. He meditated upon those eyes as his steps led him closer to the English village. Somehow a pebble from the dirt path found its way into his shoe and lodged between his stocking and his shoe, under his big toe. The pebble bit into his toe, nearly causing Creasy to take the name of the Lord in vain. He limped on a few steps so that he could lean upon a tree and remove his shoe. As he bent over, a stone whizzed over his head, smashing into the tree with such force that a piece of bark flew loose. Creasy straightened in time to see the bushes across the way rustle and tremble.

"Pernicious brats!" he called out, shaking a fist. "I'll tell your fathers!" For a moment he considered banning all slings in New England but then he recollected that King David as a boy played with a sling and the incident passed quickly from his mind, so that he made no mention of it when he reached Tom Tiley's house.

It was only the next morning when Judith brought it back to his mind.

"Are you wearing the leather bag I gave you?" She set a plate of venison scallops down before him on the table.

He thought her tone unusually sharp for such a good-natured young woman. "Um, yes," he said, pulling the leather bag from beneath his collar and listing it for her inspection.

"That's good." She nodded, satisfied.

"And it saved me!" Creasy smiled up at her, his tone light. "Some children threw a stone at me but they missed. Disrespectful brats." He resumed his breakfast, taking up a piece of golden johnnycake. This morning the cake had added bits of red cranberry. Really, Judith was a wonder of a cook, always surpassing herself with a new treat.

Judith froze where she stood. "Where was this?"

"Why, about halfway to the village," he said, stuffing his mouth.

A knock on the door brought a note to Creasy from Hetty requesting his presence in Silver Springs. He thought idly about dawdling and even refusing the summons, but it would result in her sending someone to fetch him. Really, the woman was insufferable sometimes. Still, she and he worked together with success to solve several murders, and they were here on Cape Cod to solve such another, so he could not turn his back on her. He thought it wise to tell Judith were he would be in case anyone from the native village needed him.

Judith retrieved his empty plate in silence. “Do you have your key?” These were the only words she addressed to him. Satisfied that he could unlock the door, she cleaned the table, straightened the bed, swept the floor and hung her apron upon a peg on the wall. She walked back to her own home and sought out her uncle Abraham.

Abraham Peacetree had learned from his ancestors the art of tracking. The young minister left an open trail. Abraham pointed out to his niece the spot where Creasy had leaned against a tree. He walked across to a clump of bushes. “Here the one waited, see the boot marks dug in the leaves? And he crushed the bushes when he ran away. I think your young man was followed here.”

“Is he in danger?” Judith bit a plump finger.

“Did you give him the medicine bag?”

“Yes,” Judith said. “I will see that he wears it.”

“Then he is safe.”

Ten

Creasy joined us for supper that evening. Cody was absent, mending his nets according to Thomas. We debated whether Creasy should walk abroad once more that evening. It was evident, I argued, that we had excited people's interest. Margery agreed that people were indeed interested but she did not think we should repeat the prank, which played upon their neighbor's fears. I could tell by the look on Creasy's face that he sympathized with Margery. He had his thin brows raised and his nose lifted in the air.

I ignored the look and went on with my plan. I addressed myself primarily to Tom Tiley. "The only persons we haven't seen yet are Daniel Freeman and his wife. I think we should visit them tonight. Will you come with us, Tom?"

Tiley frowned even as he nodded his head in agreement to the request. "I can't see Daniel stabbing Charlie Pierce in the back. The two were good friends."

"Someone said he had a temper." I would disclose no names.

Tom Tiley set down his wooden spoon and pushed away his trencher. "Daniel is quick with his fists—he'd be the first man to admit it—but he'd not stab any man in the back." His long face grew flushed.

Margery rose. "I'll clear the table. I shan't go with you, but Tom, you take them over. You'd best leave soon before the Freemans go to bed."

Her interruption proved a welcome relief. We all stood from

our benches. Tom was a tall man with strong arms yet he was clearly controlled by his sister. It was Margery who had composed and written the letter to Cotton Mather. Tom had just signed his name as directed by her. I'd heard her scold the big man into washing his face and hands at the pump before he entered the house. Tiley was dressed now in a clean linen shirt of her making.

Creasy turned to Margery, all smiles and conciliation. "I'll stay with you, Mistress Mason, if you please." To me he nodded. "You don't need me to walk the beach tonight," he said, his tone challenging me to dispute his decision at my peril.

I shrugged. Perhaps it was best if Margery were to have his company and protection. If Creasy fell under the lively spell of Margery Mason's dark eyes it wasn't me he'd have to answer to, it was the muscular arms and broad chest of Cody Jewett.

Daniel Freeman proved to be a man of average height with undistinguished features except for a pair of hazel eyes with black lashes that curled thick and lush as any woman must envy. His wife Sally was plump of figure, bright eyed and pink-cheeked. I liked her at once. Since it was obvious they were ready to retire for the evening I was short and forthright with my questions. I addressed them to Daniel.

"Do you know of anyone would have reason to harm Charlie Pierce?"

Daniel considered before he nodded his head in the negative. It was Sally whose cheeks flushed and whose eyes sparkled with a dangerous fire.

"Just you let me get my hands upon him, whoever did this to poor Charlie as never harmed a fly. I don't believe in such things as saints as is too Popish for my faith, but if ever there was a sainted man who helped the poor and needy it was Charlie Pierce." She waved a plump fist in the air, her rosy lips pursed.

"We've sent our eldest son out to Barnstable for the constable," Daniel said, his voice solemn.

"Yes, but we won't wait on the constable to catch this fiend." Sally's voice was firm and assured. She addressed Tom Tiley.

"You just send word to us if you find out who did this. We'll take care of him."

So Daniel Freeman had the temper? I thought his wife Sally was the more dangerous of the two. A rolling pin in the hands of such a woman was as deadly as a musket, and more reliable. I thanked them for speaking to us and we took our leave.

Tom Tiley was not a loquacious fellow so we walked in silence back to the cottage. At the door I felt the need to think further upon the events of the day and the people we'd met. I'd never sleep if I retired with all my thoughts in a muddle like this. Yes, it seemed like everyone liked Charlie Pierce, yet he'd been murdered. There must be a reason for it! I'd have to look further. Should I make Creasy dress in his ghostly costume and walk abroad again? Should I have brought Creasy with us when we'd made those visits? He was trained in the ministry to search out the guilty secrets of the human soul, and every man, woman and beast had some guilty secrets to conceal. Yet Creasy was susceptible to a pretty face, his sympathy all for women. I thought that the women we'd spoken to would respond more openly to Margery and me but perhaps I was mistaken. Creasy would no doubt kneel and pray with each in private and adjure them to confess their sins—but would he share those confessions with us? Could he even share them under his religious training? I'd have to ask him about that. Even my cousin's husband, Cotton Mather, would not reveal what was told to him in private prayers. I suspected that Cousin Cotton knew the names of one or two witches in Boston that he never revealed to the magistrates during that horrid business in Salem two years ago. I must think upon this new problem.

Tiley was speaking to me, I realized with a start. "I don't like to leave you," he said. "I shouldn't like to leave you by yourself at night."

I waved him away. "There has only been the one incident, Tom. I'm perfectly safe just walking the beach for a short while.

I shan't stray far. There are matters I have to ponder and walking on the beach is restful to me."

I suspected that Tom Tiley was not used to pondering. He gave one nod and opened the door to the cottage. "I'll just see young Mister Cotton back to the natives then."

"Yes," I said, waving him inside. I took off in the direction of the beach before the door closed upon him. Creasy would insist upon accompanying me and I did not want Creasy Cotton interfering with my cogitations—he had an annoying habit of contradicting me. We'd end up arguing instead of cogitating.

The gentle lapping of the waves along the shore was soothing as I strolled in bare feet on the sands. I'd taken my boots off and left them on the path. A harvest moon shone bright so I could avoid the slippery ribbons of amber seaweed left behind to mark the tide line. Billingsgate down by the docks had a reputation as a rowdy place where drunken sailors cavorted but here on the beach it was as peaceful as a sleeping babe. The golden sands went on in a crescent shape for nearly a mile. I scolded myself into setting aside thoughts of a certain Huguenot refugee and of concentrating on the problem at hand; namely whether Daniel Freeman had temper enough to kill his friend Mister Pierce, but I liked the man and his wife. I kicked up sand with a savage flick of my bare toes. The night is too beautiful to waste on ponderous thought, I told myself. And why not spend it dreaming of gray eyes that sparkled with laughter at a woman, and an aristocratic nose and long mouth just meant for kissing…

I heard a sound. I spun around. Had Creasy followed me? I'd kick sand right in his face if he dared. But the sound came before me, not after me, as a soft noise again reached my ears. What could it be? A beached fish—a porpoise, perhaps? The sound was curiously like a moan. I hurried forward. The moon shone in silver streaks across the soft waves. The gentle ocean turned my toes to ice as I waded in. I felt the icy cold rise up my limbs. My instincts were to back up and find the dry sand welcoming my wet feet.

"Who's there?"

Another groan was my only answer. I strained my eyes to see; I began an awkward lope with the waves dragging at the hems of my skirts. I repeated my cry. A shapeless black mass lay ahead of me, I could make out that much. A porpoise? The creatures were almost human and my sailors were superstitious of them. My arms were covered in goose bumps but not from the icy waters. My sailors told stories of half-human creatures that turned into men on land but were turned back into sea creatures in the ocean waters. Was this such a creature? Mad thoughts ran through my head as I splashed forward.

I stopped short by the black form and discovered it to be a man, bound hand and foot by rope and in dire threat to drown by the tides. All of a sudden there was a buzzing noise in my head; my brain felt numb and stuffed with cotton as in a nightmare. This could not be real! I grabbed the rope that bound the man and with both hands pulled towards the beach, timing my pulls with the incoming tide. Too soon it would reverse itself and drag the helpless man out to sea, as someone no doubt planned. I had no time to speculate as it took all my strength to drag the body up to the amber weeds that marked high tide. I nearly slipped. Once past the weeds I deemed him safe. I knelt down, digging into my pocket for the pair of sharp shears I kept there. Upon more than one occasion the shears had come in handy. Now I opened them and began to use the edges to cut through the rope that bound the man. The man groaned and I looked down at the white face to reassure him.

"Good Lord! Cody! What happened?" The words escaped me before I could think.

Cody Jewett was in no condition to speak. I took the edge of my gown and dabbed at his face. The cloth come back with black stains that I was certain must be blood. The poor man was shivering with some violence, jerking like a poppet on a string. I glanced around me but what could I do? I could not leave him on the beach while I ran for help in case the murderer came back, for an attempt at murder it clearly was meant. The man was no doubt liable to take a fit. He must be kept warm and there was no time to build a fire, even had I the means to light it. Well, I knew several ways to light a fire without the help of a warm coal but that would take precious time. I lay down upon him, spreading my light cloak over us as best I could and wrapping my arms about him. The icy cold of his body made me shiver but I held him close. Eventually his shivering subsided. Oddly enough, I think I dozed. I woke with a start when two strong arms wrapped themselves around me and a husky voice spoke into my ear.

"I thought to have the pleasure of laying on top of you, but this will do."

"Cody!" I tried to jump up but the arms held me close.

"Ouch! What did you do to my head?"

"Nothing. It wasn't me, you fool," I said, quite indignant at being accused when I had clearly rescued the man. "I saved you from being dragged out to sea."

"A likely story. You feel good. Kiss me." He tried to raise his head but it fell back into the sand. "Ouch! My head hurts like the devil." He took a deep breath. "You'd better get off me—I don't feel so good."

"I'll get off you as soon as you let me go," I said, nettled. At the release of his arms I rolled off him. No sooner had I escaped but that he turned his head and vomited into the sand.

"Did I drink too much?"

At his gasp I pulled out a handkerchief, handing it to him so that he could wipe his mouth.

"No. At least I think not, although you may have for all I know. Someone tried to kill you. They must have hit you over the head then tied you up and left you to the mercy of the tides." I scrambled to my knees and held out my hand. "Come, we'd better go before he gets back and tries again." I found a piece of rope at my feet and lifted it so that he could see. "Lucky for you I came along and I have a pair of shears I used to cut you free."

"Oh God, I'm dizzy." He attempted to raise himself upon his arms.

I knelt beside him and helped to lift him into a sitting position.

"Come on, we've got to get out of here. My scissors aren't much of a weapon." I also wanted to get Cody's head examined—for medical purposes.

"My head hurts," he said. He rose to his feet and leaned upon my shoulder.

His was a solid weight and I thanked the Lord that I had the strength to take the burden. We stumbled forward, me urging him on even as I attempted to keep the panic from my voice. I did not even stop to procure my boots, so anxious was I to leave the accursed spot. We lurched on down a sandy path through the grasses, my heart gladdening when I saw the first cottage light signifying aid and safety. It was the home of Annie Wixam and I was thankful for I knew she was not the murderer. I was also thankful the elderly do not sleep as soundly as the young. It was a strange hour to be calling.

Annie answered the door at my frantic knocking. Cody leant against the doorsill, barely able to stand at this point. Annie said not a word but wrapped her brawny arms around Cody and dragged him inside, carrying him to a bench in front of the hearth. He slumped there, head lowered. I could now see a bloodied lump behind one ear. I took a stool opposite him, glad to be relieved of my burden in more than one way.

Annie bustled around, returning with a bowl of water and a pile of cloths, some of which she used to wipe Cody's crusted head free of blood. The bowl's contents turned red. She smeared a balm on his wounds and scratches.

"What's in that?" I asked, my curiosity aroused. We each have our favorite herbal remedies and I am always quick to study new medicines for use on my sailors when mishaps occur aboard ship.

She named several herbs, the only one that surprised me being the addition of bear grease. "The natives bring it to me." Her fingers were deft in spite of Cody's protests. Soon his head was wrapped in a swath of bandages so that he looked like a half-done mummy, or more likely a skunk, with his black hair crossed by white stripes of bandage. The latter image I prayed the Lord to forgive me for my uncharitable thoughts. Really, it was no laughing matter.

"Someone tried to kill you," I said to the man. "Do you have any idea who did this?"

Cody shook his head and then groaned at the effort. He eyes were reddened and dull.

"Looks like someone hit you with a shovel," Annie said. "Good thing you were born with a hard head."

"Someone hit him hard enough to knock him unconscious," I said. "Then they tied him up and left him to drown as the tides came in. That's how I found him." I turned to Annie. "Who would do such a dastardly act? Does he have many enemies?"

"None who wouldn't brawl with him to his face, not sneak behind his back. No more than Charlie Pierce. All it takes is one bad apple, and it seems we have a rotten one in our harvest." She gave her patient a hearty pound upon the shoulder. "Now you just get undressed and hop into my bed." Her rough hands tugged at his wet shirt, pulling it over his head in spite of his feeble protests. "I've a nightshirt from my late husband that'll do." She pulled a shirt from the pile of linen she'd brought and draped it over his head. "That's it. Now get in there." She took his arm and lifted him bodily off the bench, dragging him over to the curtained bed in a corner of the room. "Take off your britches and crawl in there."

From the rustling noises I heard, Cody followed her orders. I kept my eyes on the embers of the fire in the hearth. Annie came back and spread a shirt and trousers on the bench to dry. "You're wet, too," she said, looking me over.

"I'll go back to Tiley's. I must let them know what happened." I rose.

Annie gave me a push that set me back on my stool. "I'll not have you out there with a murderer lurking about. I'll not have that on my conscience. The boy is dead to the world. He's asleep now, and even if he warn't, he's as helpless as a babe in arms. No need for a bundling board. Climb into that bed, and no one's to know if you don't tell them. Just you take off those wet clothes of yours and I'll dry them as best I can."

I was too exhausted to argue. As I thought about it, I did not want to go back out in that night with a killer near. I began to wriggle out of my robe and wet petticoats. "Where will you sleep?" I asked. I could have slept on the floor before the fire; it wouldn't have been the first time.

"I'm an old lady. Old ladies don't sleep. I'll sit up with my pitchfork for company and you needn't worry about a thing. I'll be watching." She bent over and picked up the garments as I dropped them.

I knew I was in safe hands. I stumbled over to the bed, grabbed the edge of a worn counterpane, pulled it over me and promptly fell asleep.

Eleven

I woke to the smell of ham sizzling and I answered the call of my stomach by jumping out of bed, wriggling into my dry and brushed clothing and stepping out to greet Annie. My feet were still bare and the floor felt cold so I hopped over to the hearth bench with a quick greeting.

"Oh, that smells so good!"

Annie handed me a plate with a large slice of ham upon it bordered by chunks of buttery potatoes. I've always had a hearty appetite and I did justice to Annie's work. It wasn't until I'd wiped my plate clean with a slice of bread that I thought about my companion for the night. I turned my head and could barely make out a bandaged head upon the pillows behind the bed curtains.

"We'll let him sleep today. That'll be the best thing for him." Annie handed me a mug of cider.

I sipped at the cider but strong though it was, it seemed to raise my spirits. "Well, I'd best go to Tileys and tell them what happened. They'll be wondering why I didn't come in last night. If you don't mind, Annie, I won't tell them that we shared the bed, Cody and I. Margery might not understand."

"Lord love you, anyone can see the man's been hurt and is helpless as a lamb." Annie said, letting out an unladylike snort.

"Yes, well Margery hasn't seen him yet."

I found my cloak hanging upon a wall peg and set it over my shoulders. First I would gather up my shoes from the beach and check out the site where I'd pulled Cody to safety. I was curious to see if there were any new footprints in the sand. In my haste I banged the door on my way out and heard a hiss like a snake come from Annie. I curst myself for my clumsiness.

I found my shoes where I'd left them and shoved them on my feet, then I scoured the beach until I found a spot where a body might have lain, judging from the indents in the sand. There were no discernable prints, the spot being dry and the wind having blown strong enough to erase them. There was a strand of rope coiled near the spot, and that I pocketed. It was ordinary rope and I did not think it would be of much help.

I turned my steps to the Tiley home. I found I was a little reluctant to face them but I didn't know why that should be. I'd rescued Cody from murder, after all. When I reached the home I didn't knock but burst in. I'd interrupted their breakfast. Margery looked up at my entrance but Tom kept on munching, fish cakes by their smell.

"Hetty! We were worried! Where were you?" Margery jumped up from her seat. "Have you had any breakfast?" she added.

"Yes, I've been at Annie Wixam's. She fed me. I've just come from there and I have to tell you that Cody Jewett is there, and well…he's not in good condition. Someone tried to kill him last night."

Tom Tiley looked up from his place. "Get Hetty some cider, Margery." His voice was calm. "Get into a fight, did he?" Tom looked at me with faint interest.

"Nothing like that," I said, taking a seat at the table. "I mean they tried to murder him."

Margery spilled a few drops of cider on the table as she handed me a mug. I found that I was quite thirsty and drank down the entire contents.

"But he's alive," Tom said. He looked at Margery's pale face, seeking to reassure her.

"Oh yes, he's alive. And he's safe at Annie's." I said this for Margery's benefit. If I'd doubted what she felt for Cody Jewett I knew now that she cared for the man.

"Well, we'll go as soon as we've finished breakfast." Tom resumed his eating. He nodded at Margery to seat herself, which she did, but I noted she only moved her cakes around on her plate without tasting them.

Tom made quick work of his meal even though he seemed unhurried. When he rose Margery was up like a flash and taking down her cloak. She was out the door before us, hurrying down the path.

I put my hand on Tom's arm to prevent him from following as quickly. "Tom, you'd best hear how I found him."

"I knew I should not have let you go about on your own last night," he said, his voice heavy with disapproval.

It was on my tongue to give a tart answer to the effect that he could not have stopped me, but I let it pass. "You must be glad because if I'd not gone out for a walk he would have drowned. Let me tell you what happened." I proceeded to give a graphic account of Cody's condition when I'd found him. "I didn't think my shears could hold off whatever weapon the killer used to whack Cody on the head. As it was, I practically had to carry Cody as far as Annie's, which was the first house I saw." I didn't bother mentioning how I'd shielded Cody with my own body before I could get him to move. It had seemed like hours, with the moon bright enough for the killer to spot us there. In reality it had probably been no more than fifteen or twenty minutes. I sincerely hoped that Cody's memory of that part of the evening had been erased, as well as the assassin's attack had been.

"Who would want to harm him, Tom? For Cody was clearly meant to die a horrible death. The killer could have just bashed in Cody's head while he lay unconscious. Who would do such a thing?" I shook my head. If anyone should know who hated Cody with such a deadly passion Tom would know.

Tom frowned down at the ground. "I can't think of any man who would kill Cody that way. They might in a fight by accident, but not that way. I don't know."

We walked on in silence. A seagull hopped on the sand

towards us, a bright black eye watching us in speculation. Did we have a crumb of bread to share or an apple core to throw away? A brown-spotted youngster landed near him but an angry flare of wings and a loud squawk chased the brash intruder away.

Gentle waves shone silver beneath a hazy morning sun. The breeze blew soft but with a bite, a warning of winter gales to come. I pulled my cloak tight about me. Tom wore an old linen shirt and breeches that came wide to his knees. He would take the boat out as soon as he'd seen his friend. He'd do the work of two men today, and for as many days as it took Cody to recover. I had a sudden inspiration and put my idea to him.

"Tom, I used to go out fishing with my brothers off Marblehead. I'd be glad to serve as crew for you while Cody is abed." I spoke in as diffident a tone as I could manage. "I'm sure that Mister Cotton would volunteer but I really believe I'd be of more help. Creasy has no experience. Besides, he's prone to get seasick."

Tom made a polite but definite refusal of my services.

I knew that many men object to having women on their boats and did not press the matter. Besides, someone would have to question again all the people I'd spoken to before. Someone must have seen something! And perhaps the attack on Cody was a response to the foolish trick we'd tried with Creasy acting the part of Pierce's ghost. Perhaps we had succeeded in frightening the killer into a reaction. Cody had certainly been a large part of the prank. I ran the possibilities through my head. Daniel Freeman might have followed us, but why attack Cody Jewett and not Tom or me? When had the attack taken place? Freeman would have had to hit Cody on the head and tie him up to drown before we questioned him, and then he would have had to rush back and prepare himself for bed before we got there... It did not seem feasible. My reaction was to blame that red fox Roach, who might have several reasons including his lovely daughter for hating Cody. I'd have to ask Cody about Lucy, if he'd ever flirted with her. But I couldn't do that in front of Margery. Perhaps Cody was in debt to Roach and couldn't pay.

Tom interrupted my thoughts. "You know, Hetty, I didn't but half like the idea of sending that letter to Mister Mather. 'Twas Margery's doing, but I'm glad to have you here. I think you can best help by asking your questions, as Margery says you do."

This was the longest speech I'd heard from the man and I felt touched. By this time we'd arrived at the home of Annie Wixam. With a brief knock we entered, to find Cody sitting up in bed eating a plate of eggs while Margery perched on the bed beside him, holding on to the sleeve of the overlarge nightshirt he wore. If her grasp interfered with Cody's feeding he showed no signs of minding. When Cody spotted Tom he handed the plate to Margery and threw back the bedclothes, ready to tumble out and dress himself for a day of fishing.

Margery, Tom and I protested with one voice. Annie stepped in, waving a big wooden spoon at the invalid. "You'll stay in bed, young man, until I tell you that you can get up. Perhaps tomorrow, lad. You'll not be of any help to Tom is you get dizzy and fall out of the boat."

"I've got a hard head, you said it yourself." Cody's protest did him little good.

"Aye, as hard-headed a fool as there is, and I've mended it after many a fight, but stay in bed one more day you will." The finality in Annie's tone brooked no argument.

Cody leaned back against the headboard of the bed, a grin creasing his face.

I noted the slight wince he gave and the pallor beneath the ruddy complexion.

Annie turned to us, the spoon held high in one large fist. "You can see he's still alive, but I'm going to change the bandage on that hard head of his and he's going back to sleep. You can come back tonight." She pointed the spoon. "That means you, too, Mistress Margery."

We waited for a reluctant Margery to join us at the door. I took advantage of her hesitancy to speak to Annie. "May I just ask him one question?" I was the one who brought him here, so

I thought I had a certain right. I waited for Annie's nod before I turned to the invalid.

"Cody, do you know who hit you last night? Did you see or hear anything? Anyone?"

Cody began to shake his head but winced at the effort. "No, I didn't see anyone. If I had, I could have defended myself. I don't remember anything. Don't even know how I got here."

I felt relief at these words. Now I need not explain to Margery how I'd sheltered him with my own body, even though it was to save his life. Some women would prefer a man to freeze to death rather than allow another woman to place her body over his. I wondered how I would feel if another woman lay on top of Alexandre, even if it was to save his life. I could not imagine any other woman laying on top of Alexandre Bernon but me, and thinking of laying on top of my French refugee lead me into flights of fantasy…

I forced myself to return to the business at hand; there was nothing for it but to go back and question everyone I'd questioned before. Only this time I'd bring Creasy Cotton with me. His training in the ministry might uncover the guilty secrets of one human soul; secrets I had not been able to expose. Creasy was exceptionally good with females. So was his cousin, Cotton Mather. There must be something about the Cotton and the Mather males that drew women like moths to a flame, but whatever it was, I remained unaffected by it. No doubt I'd been overexposed to their masculine charms.

Twelve

A note to Creasy brought him to Tiley's unpretentious home. Margery busied herself with baking and packing food into a basket, meant for the invalid at Annie's. She quite ignored Creasy's ogling. As we walked out the door Tom carried the basket and Margery hurried before him. I was able to walk with Creasy and to regale him with my adventure of the night before.

"How fortunate you found the man, Hetty!" He grasped my hand in his long fingers. "You showed great bravery and good sense."

I felt relieved that he did not condemn me for lying on top of Cody's body to keep him warm. Creasy was something of a healer, as were most ministers, not only with spiritual advice but with herbs and salves as well. He understood and approved my conduct.

"It must have been a terrifying ordeal," he said with clear sympathy in his voice.

I hadn't thought about it in those terms until he said it, but suddenly my knees began to shake and my steps to wobble. It had been a terrifying ordeal! I felt nauseous all of a sudden and was forced to seat myself upon the nearest log. I took deep breaths until my innards felt a bit more composed.

Creasy seated himself beside me. "I'm very proud of you, Hetty. You did well to remain with him at Mistress Wixam's home, too. She might well have needed you to fetch a doctor for the man."

"A doctor? Annie Wixam is the only healer here, Creasy. She wouldn't let me go out by myself, either. Do you forget there was a murderer on the loose last night?" 'Men,' thought I! 'Not an ounce of common sense amongst 'em.' I did not find it reassuring that my friend and companion in murder investigations would have blithely sent me out into the night to have my head chopped off.

Creasy raised his knobby hands in protest. "I didn't mean that, Hetty. I wasn't thinking."

I sniffed. "Well you'd better start thinking, Creasy Cotton, because you are going to have to question everyone that Margery and I spoke to before. Perhaps you'll get more out of them than we did." I spread my skirts and straightened my legs. My breathing returned to normal. The sun warmed my face and a soft breeze stirred my skirts. I closed my eyes. A sense of relief flooded through me. I did not have to bear the burden of this investigation any longer.

"Now you've got two objects to uncover, the murder of Charlie Pierce and the attempted drowning of Cody Jewett. You'll have to come out of hiding but I doubt there's a need for it any longer—using you for a ghost, that is," I said.

"I'm glad of that. I didn't like wearing the dead man's clothing." Creasy frowned. "Don't you believe the two are related? Done by the same hand?"

I nodded. "But we must keep an open mind." I sat up straight as a thought occurred to me. "Do you think your night walks were responsible for the attack upon Cody?"

Creasy considered the question for a moment. "That depends. Does Cody have any enemies? He seems a caustic kind of fellow."

"He is caustic," I said, "but Tom says that the men he knows would fight in the open. They wouldn't think to tie him up and leave him to drown. That takes a devious kind of villain, so I think."

Creasy gazed down his aristocratic nose, regarding me with a touch of pity. "I'm afraid we unleashed havoc with that prank, Hetty. We must all take care at this point, and that includes you.

Please don't walk abroad by yourself any longer, Hetty. I beg you to heed me on this."

His tone was so sincere I could not but honor his concern and vow to keep a companion with me while I remained at Billingsgate. In many instances his concerns set up my back so that I would go and do the opposite of what he desired, but this time I would heed his advice. My spirits sunk as I considered that an idea of mine should have caused so much hurt to Cody—and by extension to both Tom and Margery. She should by rights be angry with me. I would understand if she refused to speak to me again. At least Margery was blameless. She'd had no part in my scheme. That I'd been the one to find Cody and to rescue him from his dire fate did not lessen my feelings of guilt. I deserved to be locked in a deep, dark dungeon where I could do no one any harm. I raised my face to the sun, hoping it's light would burn away my sins.

Creasy interrupted my repentant thoughts. "Why don't we begin the questioning now? I'm free and not in disguise any longer. I'd as soon get it done. The sooner we find the fiend who's making these attacks the sooner we can return to Boston."

"Oh, I wish we were home!" I spoke involuntarily. Just the mention of the city and I longed to be there where I had nothing more to deal with than conniving merchants, drunken sailors and what to wear for a dinner with Alexandre Bernon, that charming Huguenot gentleman. I knew my ship, the *Anhinga,* would return to Billingsgate soon for another cargo of oysters. I longed to board it and sail away from Billingsgate harbor forever. However, what I would do in actuality was to borrow Iron John from the crew to act as my guard. He's not called Iron John for nothing.

Creasy reached out his hand and helped me to my feet.

We began our questioning with Mistress Abitha Cole and her young boy. She opened at our knock upon her door and it seemed her face brightened at our sight. She waved us inside. The walls of her cottage were remained a dingy white, but the table had been polished so that it shone, and two stools were newly cushioned with embroidered covers. I hoped that the coin I'd given her boy had been put to good use. She waved us on to the stools.

I noted a spinning wheel on the other side of the hearth and beyond that a bed with green harrateen hangings. A heavy chest stood at the foot of the bed.

"Oh, I'm so glad you've come!" She clasped her bony hands together. Her little boy hung back, peeping at us from behind her skirts. "I did not know what to do, and that's the truth."

I waved to the little boy. Mistress Cole caught my greeting. She reached behind her and grasped the boy by the arm, pulling him forward. "My Jackie is a good boy and he's been taught his bible and to obey the Lord and his elders, but I'm afraid he's done something naughty… Well, I knew the way he was acting that he'd done something as he shouldn't, but he wouldn't tell me. So I looked around where he might hide things and finally found it under the mattress of his little bed." Mistress Cole walked over to the mantle as she spoke, poking her hand behind a pewter plate. She turned back to us with a sharp knife in her hands.

I almost jumped from my stool, ready to run, so certain was I we'd found the murderer, but the woman took great care to present the knife to Creasy handle-first. Calming my nerves, I noted the handle of lovely mother-of-pearl.

"You can see how shiny it is. I think that's what attracted my Jackie to it. He told me he found it in the dead man's back. I think it's the knife that killed Charlie Pierce." She paused with a worried look upon her thin face. "I hope no charges will be brought against my little boy! Truly, he did not know he was doing wrong…" The woman looked with appeal at Creasy. "I was out clamming that morning, near where they found the body. Jackie was with me. He found the body and saw the shiny handle of the knife. He took it out and hid it in his shirt. I only just found it this morning and I was in such a dither wondering what to do!"

"Of course there will be no charges against the little lad, Mistress," Creasy said, with his most sympathetic expression, the one he put on for grieving widows. "No harm shall come to him. Why he's a fine, strong lad!" Creasy beamed with good will at the boy. "He shall have a reward for finding the knife. Have you got a penny, Hetty?"

Creasy reached out his hand to me and I dug through my pocket for a coin. I brought out several and Creasy selected two of the shiniest pennies. He offered them to the boy, who grabbed them and disappeared behind his mother's skirts.

"Thank you, sir. This is such a relief to me! I did not know what to do with that knife."

I nudged my companion, mouthing 'Ask her of Cody!' before he gave away my whole fortune.

"Ummm—Mistress Cole, can you tell me of anyone who might have wished to kill Cody Jewett? It seems that someone tried to make away with him last night."

"Cody?" The woman appeared startled, her eyes opening wide and creases appearing in her high forehead. "Someone tried to kill Cody?"

"Yes," I said before Creasy could speak. I did not want to tell the woman of the manner that was planned for Cody's death. If she knew any details it was either through speedy gossip or she was the one who made the attempt.

"Well…Cody Jewett is a quick man with his fists, that's so, and he's gotten into fights with the other men around here." She spoke in a slow tone, considering the question. "But he's as fast as Charlie Pierce to offer help when a man needs it. Did he get into another fight last night?"

"Did he escort women to functions like Pierce did?" I asked, ignoring her question. I studied her face, thin and long with green eyes like a cat, her brown hair straggling and pulled back from her face with a black ribbon.

Her gaze did not waver under mine. "No, not to my knowing. Cody is a bold fellow and women would not trust him. Nor husbands," she added.

"So he would have enemies," I said.

The thin brows crinkled in concentration. "No, not enemies, exactly. I would not say enemies. We are a small community here—

we help each other as best we can. Cody does his part and we all know we can count upon him for help. Cody's a strong swimmer and has saved more than one from drowning. The waves are rough beyond the bay here. As for fights, why all the men fight when they drink too much. 'Tis what a man does in his cups, and there is precious little to do with their time once they've fished all day. Mind you, I don't condone it, but so it goes." She pushed a stray strand of hair from her face.

I released a sigh of vexation, I could not help it. So people depended upon Cody Jewett and everyone liked Charlie Pierce. Then who killed the one and tried to kill the other? Had the two men seen something not meant for their eyes? I had few doubts that there was smuggling going on amidst the twist and turns of the Cape coastline but Billingsgate wasn't known to me as a smuggler's paradise. I had eyes all over the New England coast. My spies would have told me so years ago. Of course there were always tales of buried treasure on the Cape. Had Pierce and Jewett stumbled upon such a cache? Then word would have spread as fast as the *Anhinga* could sail from Boston to Hog Island. There is no way you could keep a treasure horde secret; nor even a hint of there being a treasure horde some place. Seekers would be out with shovels within minutes of such a rumor. There was something about a buried treasure that proved an irresistible lure.

I reminded Creasy that we had other people to see. We stood and took our leave of the woman and her little boy.

With the knife safely wrapped in his pocket, I directed Creasy to the home of Robert Roach. He'd said he could identify the knife if we found it, so perhaps he could identify the killer. This was our best hope so far. I told Creasy what I knew of the man and his family, attempting to keep my dislike of the man from my voice. There was just something about that foxy face I could not trust.

Roach was home, ensconced in the bosom of his family. Creasy's eyes gleamed at sight of daughter Lucy's blond curls and sweet smile. Madame Roach rose as I introduced him as Mr. Increase Cotton, cousin of Mister Cotton Mather of Boston. She simpered, making a deep curtsey, which Creasy returned with an unnecessarily deep bow—at least it was too low in my opinion, but then Creasy does like to play the gentleman. Robert Roach merely bent his fox-colored head to acknowledge the introduction.

Madame turned to her daughter. "Lucy, get the silver service and bring a dish of tea for our guests."

I was surprised that she included me as a guest. Creasy, however, raised his hand and declined the offer. "We shan't be able to accept your hospitality this time, but thank you for the offer, and I trust we may enjoy your company at another time, under more pleasant circumstances. You see," he turned to Robert Roach as he spoke, "we wonder if you can identify this object." His hand went into his coat pocket, retrieving a linen-wrapped parcel. With great care he uncovered the object. It lay in his extended hand with a soft sheen and deadly shape.

"Yes. That's Charlie Pierce's knife," Roach said.

Thirteen

We were disappointed to learn that the knife was Charlie Pierce's own weapon. Here we'd thought we'd found the clue to the killer's identity. The knife was certainly not a poor fisherman's weapon, that much we'd realized with the mother-of-pearl handle. It wasn't a knife that would be used to gut fish. A pretty thing, Roach suggested it might be of Spanish or Italian manufacture. He did not know it's history or how Pierce came to possess it, but he knew it belonged to Pierce.

"By the way," Roach added, "your ship has docked. My clerk just brought me a message. I like to keep an eye on the comings and goings about the docks—it gives me an advantage in my dealings."

I nodded and thanked the man as we took our leave. I had other business to conduct besides murder and it was time I gave some attention to my mercantile affairs. Justice was uppermost, of course, as my late husband and magistrate Mister Henry would say, but business gave me the means to conduct my investigations.

"Well, Creasy," I said, "I'll take care of some affairs aboard ship this evening, but perhaps you could ask Tom or Margery to take you to visit the Mayos and the Freemans with you. Perhaps you may be able to squeeze information from them that I couldn't get. Perhaps they might recall something relevant since I spoke to them. What with the attack upon poor Cody last night they might be jarred into considering my questions with a bit more care." Not that the couples were unwelcoming when I'd questioned them, but new events may have jogged their memories, so I thought and so I hoped.

"We are about to meet the Warren's, next." I motioned to the hut with the broken shutters.

"The man I frightened pretending to be a ghost?" Creasy frowned, his thin black brows gathering like birds of prey. "I feel quite guilty about that, Hetty. It wasn't right."

"Yes, well it worked. We needed to get out word that Pierce's spirit walked abroad to stir up the guilty party's conscience and that attack upon Cody Jewett was one result. I'm sure they were connected." I laid my hand upon Creasy's coat sleeve. "Jack Warren is a born gossip. In the old days he would have been put in the stocks and been pelted with rotten apples. And I would have been the first to throw one."

"He is a human being, Hetty, and we know to treat sinners in a more merciful manner these days." Creasy lectured as he knocked upon the door.

"Don't forget to ask him about the attack upon Cody Jewett," I said in a whisper.

A head with hair bristling like a porcupine answered Creasy's knock, peeping around the door. I noted a fresh bruise below one eye, the skin beginning to turn purple. The door opened wide enough to allow us to enter.

"I thought you were my wife," Warren greeted us. "She's gone to her mother's again."

I introduced Creasy as Mister Increase Cotton, a minister from Boston.

"Oh, sir, would you pray with me?" Warren clasped together his thick hands. He nearly bounced in his excitement. "I don't know what to do. These are sinful times, what with murder and beatings and such. Not that Cody Jewett is innocent, exactly, for we are all of us sinners, but if a big man like Jewett can be struck down with a club we are none of us safe! My wife is sore afraid so she has gone to her mother's house as is on Chequesset Neck and out of the violence of Billingsgate. And I have a confession to make—I am glad she has left me. I think to take a new wife, you know. There were some rough sailors harassing a young woman down by the docks so I interfered and offered to walk the young woman to her home, which I did and she was much taken with me, I must say. Mary hit me when she heard about it." He raised a broad finger to touch gingerly beneath his eye.

Creasy readily agreed to pray with the man, but before he could enter the hut I made my excuses, only pausing to ask Warren if he knew of anyone who might hate Jewett enough to attack him from behind.

To give the man credit, Warren thought for several moments before he spoke. "Cody Jewett has a sharp tongue. Why, he calls me and my wife names all the time—'simpletons' and I don't know what else. And he's loose with women. Well, I won't name any names but there's more than one husband as has reason to fight Cody Jewett—except he's a hard fighter, is Cody. If it were me, I would tackle him from behind, but I didn't do it. Wouldn't do it at all."

That seemed to me an honest reaction. I thought the man too much of a coward to make an attempt on Jewett's life. I left the two men to their prayers.

Back in my tiny office on the *Anhinga* I opened the correspondence that lay in a neat pile waiting for my attention. I sifted through the letters before choosing one in particular. The letter was written in a hand very dear to me. The words of endearment that greeted me were rendered painful by the information that Alexandre Bernon had set sail for England on business related to family lands. Since his family lands were located in France, I had no doubt he would sneak himself into France where Huguenots were executed without trial and get himself hanged or worse.

"The fool!" I cried this out loud as I dropped the paper to the floor. The rest of my letters I ignored, deciding instead to keep myself busy supervising the loading of casks of oysters. New England markets would take all the casks I could fit into my ship, of such value were the Billingsgate crop. They were tasty little creatures made so by the replenishing tides of the bay. Tides. I shivered at the thought of what those tides might have done to a body bound with rope and helpless.

Not that my supervision was needed, for I hired a capable crew, but it might take my mind off what I felt was Alexandre's betrayal. How could I regard this as anything but betrayal when the man for whom I hungered set sail without me? Would I have done that to him? No, I would not. I'd even thought to coax him to visit me on Cape Cod, carrying him to me on my own ship.

I watched as the casks were lifted on board my ship. Billingsgate oysters keep well in casks and they are a favorite with diners in Boston and in other cities of New England and beyond. I heard my name called and turned to find Cody Jewett approaching me. I noted a small bit of plaster on the back of his head, otherwise he looked his old bold self. He stopped by my side.

"A word with you, Hetty?"

I nodded and we walked away from the ship. Not until we were well out of the crew's hearing did we speak. I broke the silence first, asking with honest curiosity. "How is your head?"

Cody's lips crinkled into a cross between a smirk and a smile. "I've a hard head. I'm fine now. It was Annie made me keep to my bed. I couldn't gainsay her—she's been good to me."

We kept on walking until he placed his broad hand upon my shoulder, stopping me well beyond sight of the ship. I looked up at him. His eyes were black and shining as coal.

"Annie told me how you saved my life, Hetty. I want to thank you." He bent his head and kissed me on the lips, a simple touch between friends.

There was a flicker of surprise in the dark eyes when I returned his touch with the full pressure of my mouth. His arms went around me, drawing me in tight against his body. He returned my kiss in full measure. It felt good to feel a man's arms around me, his mouth pressing against mine. I have a woman's needs, after all, ship owner or no.

We stood in that embrace for several moments until he

released me with a sudden drop of his arms. Cody grabbed my wrist and pulled me after him. I had to run to keep up with his long strides. He led me to his cabin and opened the door. I barely had time to note how neat the place looked, with a table and stools on one side of the hearth and pots and pans standing in orderly rows on the other side. Fishing nets covered one wall on the far side. There was a faint odor of fish in the place but all the homes in Billingsgate held such an odor.

The bolt slammed behind me, my cloak fell to the floor with a push from his quick fingers, my robe falling beside it just as swiftly. I shimmied out of my petticoats by myself as Cody divested himself of his shirt and small clothes. Cody carried me in my shift to a large bed hung with curtains of green harrateen, which hangings he thrust aside and tossed me onto the bed. Our lovemaking was explosive and brief, neither one of us wanted to dally. Afterwards I lay in his arms, idly playing with the sparse black hairs on his broad chest. His skin was white as milk where the sun had not touched it. He smelled of perspiration and of lye soap, a male scent.

Cody divested me of a very wrinkled shift. I was glad it was not my best lace garment. He untied the ribbon that held my hair in place and spread strands around my naked bosoms.

"You've hair the color of new honey," he said. "It's beautiful. Your bosoms are beautiful, too."

He bent over me and fixed his mouth to one, suckling there like a hungry babe. His left hand sought and held the other globe while his right hand slid between my thighs, rubbing gently so that I gasped aloud with pleasure. He had me quivering like a calves-foot jelly and begging for release, which he finally gave me in long, slow strokes. He pulled himself out, looming over me like a great bear.

"You're my woman now. Say it," he commanded.

"I'm your woman," I said, fascinated by his bold eyes.

"You belong to me. Say it."

"I belong to you."

I would have said anything so that we could find fruition together, which we did with groans and cries of pleasure. Stuck far back in my brain was a niggardly rebellion that tried to convince me I was commander of my own person, but I paid it no heed.

We lay side by side for perhaps ten minutes until my own lust rose again and I decided I would make love to him. Using the bosoms he so admired I ran them over his body from head nearly to toe, except that when I reached his nether regions he became so rigid he begged me for release.

I nearly asked him to repeat the words, "I'm your man, you belong to me," but decided it might seem like mockery. Instead I flung my legs over his belly and seated myself upon him. His groans were music to me. Sated, I rolled over beside him for a brief nap.

We were not through with our romp, however, for he pulled off one of the fringed cords that held back the bed hangings and wrapped it around my wrists. He tied me to the bedpost and began the most exquisite torture I'd ever experienced, twisting, suckling and tugging upon me until I felt I would go mad. I fought to break my bonds, biting and kicking whatever portion of his body came within my reach. My nipples were as rigid as wooden pegs. Cody merely grinned down at me, his black eyes gleaming. Every part of my body ached when he was done, but it was such a pleasurable ache I could only forgive the man. I lay by his side as limp as a sack of pillows.

I must have napped once again for Cody woke me with a wet towel across my abdomen, motioning to a basin of water on a small stand by the bed. He laid my clothes on the bed. My arms were free of restraint, I noted, not without a pang of regret. I also noted that the room was very dark. I forced myself to rise and to dress.

"I'll walk you back to the ship," Cody said. "I don't want you out there alone in the night."

"What about you?" I struggled into my petticoats. "You were the one who was attacked. Who's going to walk you back?" I could, of course, assign a sailor or two for the job but no doubt he would be insulted. Men. Never can they admit to being less than an Achilles.

"I'm on my guard now, it won't happen again," he said. "I carry a knife at all times."

I finished dressing and we left by the front door. If Cody looked to see if anyone noticed us leaving his house together, I did not see him do so. He seemed confident and uncaring whether anyone saw us together.

"Do you want to stop at Annie's? She'll feed us, and no questions asked."

I shook my head. "I've a cook on board. He'll give me something to eat when I'm hungry."

Cody stopped. He flicked a finger under my chin. "You were hungry a few minutes ago. Ready to devour me, I swear."

I ducked beneath his hand. A change of subject was needed, I thought. "Cody, do you remember anything before you were attacked? Anything at all? A sound, a smell…"

Cody frowned in thought. We continued our walk.

"No sound, or I would have turned. Smell? It all smells like dead fish down there. I don't remember anything. I don't even remember going down to the beach, but I know I'd checked my gear in the boat for the next day. I always do that."

"Do you remember walking to Annie's with me?" I felt a small shudder pass over my arms at the thought of that walk, when I was afraid the killer would strike at us and me with only a pair of shears to stop him.

"No, I don't remember anything except waking up in Annie's bed with my head on fire. Annie told me you brought me there. That's why I came to thank you." His eyes gleamed. "I hope I thanked you properly. Four times, I believe."

I felt my face flush. "Annie's was the first house I came to," I said, attempting to keep the conversation away from intimacy. "Anything you may remember, no matter how small, may be a clue to the killer's identity. The way you were tied up and left to drown means that you have an enemy who hates you. This was a personal attack. Who hates you so much, Cody?"

Cody only shook his head. "The men I know may dislike me but they would strike me to my face, not my back. I can't think of anyone who would hit me from behind. Not one. And who would hate Charlie Pierce? There's not a better man than Charlie was."

"And someone stabbed him in the back. Are we talking about a jealous husband for either one of you?" I watched his face.

"Maybe for me… But still, they'd fight me from head on. And Charlie, well, no husband ever complained about Charlie. The wives wouldn't let them. Charlie was a gentleman."

A dead gentleman, thought I, but I kept the thought to myself. "A jealous father, perhaps? Say, Robert Roach? Did you ever flirt…with Lucy Roach?"

"Lucy? The likes of a poor fisherman for young Lucy Roach? I should say not. Now the mother, that's another matter. Ellen Roach would hump me in a minute, if I let her." He spoke without bragging, but in a matter of fact voice.

His answer relieved me in several ways. I wasn't exactly jealous but Lucy was so much younger than me. As for Mary's mother, well, Ellen was as much competition as a mangy old dog.

Fourteen

Creasy lingered over his breakfast, knowing he had a late morning appointment to meet Hetty on board her ship. A dish of oyster fritters, a bowl of steamed cod and a platter of Indian fry cakes kept him occupied until he felt sated from his meal and he noticed that Judith was unusually silent. Missing was her flow of cheery remarks as she cooked and served him. Poor girl, he'd paid her hardly any attention spending so much time at Tom Tiley's home and going about Silver Springs questioning people. Really, she was a gem of a cook, and she hadn't tried any of her bedroom tricks since that one night. He should have been aware that native women gave their favors freely as a matter of friendliness. Perhaps he'd been a trifle harsh in his rejection of her, although he did not regret that action. He decided to compliment her on her cooking. She seemed pleased when he thought to do that. This time, however, she was indifferent, as if her mind was on other things.

Judith gave him a sharp look. "Are you wearing the leather bag I gave to you?"

"Yes." To placate her he pulled the little sack from beneath his shirt and held it up for her to see.

"Good. See that you keep it on."

That was her only comment to him. Creasy had a mind to chide her for her heathen superstitions but he put off his scold for another time. He'd catch her in a better mood. After all, she hadn't asked him to bow down and worship a heathen idol. If wearing a small leather bag of herbs found favor with her he was almost obligated to wear it. No doubt it was for his health's sake. Herbs were of great medicinal value; no one knew that better than Cousin Cotton Mather, who intended to write a book about it. Well, Cousin Cotton wrote books about everything, come to that. Creasy had often wondered how he found the time. Writing out a proper sermon took him hours of careful planning whereas Cotton had a head full of sermons. Creasy pushed back his chair to take his leave. Hetty valued promptness and he'd as soon arrive early as late.

Although Judith believed in her uncle's powers she disliked the idea that Creasy was being followed and that he'd even been attacked once. She'd taken to following him herself when he left the village, until she made certain he was unobserved by anyone but herself. This morning she knew of his appointment to visit the Boston lady, his friend. Judith knew there was nothing but friendship between the two of them. She felt no pangs of jealousy as she did when he paid a visit to Tom Tiley's sister. But then she also knew that the fisherman Cody claimed that sister and Cody was a very strong man. That contest was like a sheep against a wolf.

Judith walked with soundless steps behind Creasy, keeping well back but knowing he would not turn his head to see if he was followed. The English were very trusting. For that matter, so were the Punonakanit but you wouldn't catch a five year old unawares if someone tried to stalk him.

When Creasy came within hailing distance of the Boston woman's big ship—she must be a rich woman to own such a vessel—Judith turned and trudged back along the beach. It would be good to gather some clams for supper. Creasy said he would be back tonight to speak to the people, who enjoyed his powerful words. Even should he dine with that Tiley woman, his preaching always gave him an appetite for food, and she always had food prepared for him. It was just unfortunate that his words did not give him an appetite for lusts of the flesh. She could have relieved that hunger, too.

Judith bent over, searching in the sand for the tiny bubbles beneath which clams lay hidden. Her fingers were quick, even without a digging tool, and she soon had a dozen clams tied up in the folds of her apron. She straightened when she heard the click of oars on the bay. A voice hailed her.

"Hey, give me a hand, will you? Pull me in."

Judith waded into the water, ignoring the cold. She caught the side of the dinghy and pulled it to shore.

The stranger jumped from the boat, an oar still clutched in one hand. "Why, it's the minister's doxie, ain't it?" Two eyes regarded her with contempt.

Judith stiffened. She did not know the meaning of the word spoken but she understood that it was meant as an insult. "I am cook to the minister," she said, her voice flat.

"Does he talk to you?" The stranger leaned forward, looming over the young woman.

"Talk to me?" Judith was puzzled. "Of course he talks to me. How else can he tell me what he wants for breakfast?"

"I mean does he talk to you like in bed? Where he goes during the day, perhaps?"

"I am not in his bed. I am his cook." Judith wished it were otherwise but she must tell the truth.

"He doesn't tell his doxie what he is doing? Does he not say that he is looking for the murderer of Charlie Pierce?" The stranger sneered.

"I do not know this." Judith frowned. "It is not what we speak of." She knew of the death of an English but nothing more than that. "I am his cook," she said, repeating her position. She looked down at the sand beneath her feet. She noted the overlarge boots of the stranger.

"Why do you follow him, then? I've seen you follow him. You followed him just now, didn't you?" It was a challenge more than a question.

"And why do you follow him? I've seen your prints." She pointed to the boots.

"Injun slut, that's the last thing you'll ever see." The stranger raised the oar and struck its blade across her head.

Judith stumbled sideways and fell to her knees in the water. A second blow knocked her flat upon her back, bubbles coming from her mouth as the gentle waves covered her face. She tried to rise but two hands pressed her back beneath the water. She could see a face contorted by the waves above her. Her mouth and her nostrils filled with water so that she couldn't breathe. The two hands were merciless, holding her down as she struggled to raise her head. A black cloud filled her brain; her arms twitched and were still.

Creasy heard the keening from a distance away. He quickened his steps and finally broke into a run. A crowd of native peoples surrounded the hut where the keening wails rose. It was the hut of Judith's mother and father. Perhaps the father had met with an accident, he thought. The family would need his comfort. Poor Judith! She was close to her father. He pushed his way through the crowd to enter the hut. The body in the coffin was not of the father but that of the young woman herself. Creasy's tears mingled with those of the father and the uncle. The mother keened on in a cry that burned Creasy's soul. He should have been there. He should have saved her. She drowned. It must have been an accident, the uncle confided to him. Judith was a good swimmer and would never think of suicide, but even strong swimmers drown, he said, his voice thick with sorrow.

Fifteen

Following an excellent night's sleep and a hearty breakfast of fried oysters, eggs, biscuits and a small piece of beef, with cider to wash it down, I sat at my desk to draw up a list of possible suspects for the murder of Charlie Pierce and the attempted murder of Cody Jewett. With a pang of conscience I remembered my friend Margery and what wrong I had done her by my romp with Cody. Of course, he had wronged her, as well, but he was a man, and faithless, only to be expected and excused. I had spared not even a thought for Margery yesterday. How could I have been so selfish? How could I have betrayed her? It was as well I slept on board my ship last night for I found I could not have looked her in the face this morning.

I would consult with Creasy as soon as he arrived. Perhaps he had uncovered some piece of information that would help solve this mystery. Soon I would have missives from Cotton Mather flying at me as to why I had not make my report to him. Why hadn't I solved the murder in this small community? What could be so difficult? Billingsgate was only a small settlement, not like Boston, the largest city in all the colonies. Mather would feel his reputation at stake, for the appeal for help had come to him and he had assigned Creasy and me to clear it up. I knew the harangues to which we should be subjected, me in particular, because I was a woman and the fair sex should keep their place. This from Cotton Mather, even though I had solved several murders, with Creasy Cotton's help, to keep the fair Bay Colony safe from sin.

I turned to my piece of paper and wrote the first name. I decided to include everyone no matter what, so the names of Tom Tiley and his sister headed the list. Of course they were the ones who called for our help, but Margery certainly had a reason to attack Cody although she may not know it and hopefully would never discover the reason, which reason took place after the attack in any event. Or perhaps Cody had strayed before—did she know about his roving eye and his roving hands? I forced myself to stop thinking of those roving hands or I'd never get anything done… Anyway, Margery was a small woman. It was doubtful she could whack Cody over the head with a shovel since she was so tiny. And Tom, what reason would he have? I crossed both names off my list.

Next I wrote the names of Jack and Mary Warren. I doubted Jack Warren would have the courage to attack a baby duckling, and his wife seemed to have moved to her mother's house. I'd have to ask how far away the mother lived from Billingsgate. I left both names on the list.

I wrote down the name of Annie Wixam and immediately crossed it off. Her weapon of choice seemed to be the pitchfork. She'd had Cody under her power for at least a night and a day and could have done away with him at any time she wished. I knew she liked Cody. Then there was Abitha Cole and her little boy but I was truly doubtful she would leave her lad alone at night to attack Cody. And why would she kill Charlie Pierce? It was the little boy who'd found the dagger. She'd turned it over to us with obvious relief. She'd been on the scene but the man was all ready dead when the boy pulled out the knife with its shiny handle. I did not cross her name off but I left a question mark beside it.

Next I wrote the names of the Roach family. Robert Roach was strong enough to hit Cody and to tie him up, but what would he gain from it? No, he'd lose a customer. Unless Cody had trifled with his daughter. It remained a possibility. I'd have to ask Cody if he had lied about a flirtation with Lucy. Madame Roach was too small in stature to strike the blow that felled a strong man like Cody Jewett… Here again I had to stop myself from dreaming about the strength in those arms and thighs—I do like a man with strong thighs. Young Lucy was taller than her mother and of a full figure. She might have the strength but she would have to dirty her pretty dress and muddy the hems from wading in the water. I could not see her doing that, not for a poor fisherman. I left her name on the list and left the name of Robert Roach because I'd taken a dislike to the man.

I wrote the names of the Freemans, man and wife, and the Mayo's as well. I would consult Creasy upon them. I even left a blank space for an unknown person. I thought we had met everyone in the little community but there could yet be someone whom we had missed.

Leaning back in my chair I perused the list. It was imperative that I find this murderer as soon as possible. Once the *Anhinga* was filled with her cargo she must sail for Boston and if I did not sail with her I would lose my bunk. I could not stay with Margery and Tom any longer, that was obvious to me. I felt too shamed. Oh, why had I succumbed to Cody Jewett's bold eyes yesterday? It was all the fault of Alexandre Bernon, who left me and sailed away to England. Only the Lord knew when I'd see him again. His image haunted me; the warm gray eyes, the aristocratic nose, that long mouth meant for kisses… I indulged myself for a few moments, then I shook my head to clear the image from it and went about my ship's business. Time enough to consider the list when Creasy came on board.

My friend appeared mid-morning. I motioned Creasy to take my chair while I moved to the bunk. I motioned to the list upon the desk.

"I'm making up a list of suspects. Did you learn anything from your visits to the Freeman's and the Mayos?" I did not beat about the bush.

Creasy slumped in the chair, turning it so that his long legs spread out. "Where you were you yesterday?"

He regarded me with a frown. His face looked tired, as if he had not slept well.

"Why, did you need me for anything?" I countered his question.

"You won't believe what happened," he said. "I told you that prank we pulled would lead to trouble, and it has. Those good people you sent me to question think that the ghost of Charlie Pierce attacked Cody Jewett. Now, why should the ghost attack his friend Cody, I asked, but they think ghosts do not recognize friend from foe. These people are afraid to go out at night lest they come upon Pierce's spirit. It's the men who are most afraid, and they've frightened their wives. What folly! It's well known that ghosts haunt those who have wronged them, not innocent people. But try and convince the Mayos and the Freemans of that. They say it must be a ghost to knock a strong man like Cody Jewett unconscious, and to tie him up and leave him to drown suggests a very malevolent ghost to them. They want no part of such a spirit."

I sighed aloud. I knew fishermen were superstitious but this beat all my notions of ghosts. Besides, the ghost was not real. Still, it had certainly stirred the community. I had no doubt the attack upon Cody was made by the murderer of Charlie Pierce. Whoever had struck Cody down struck in hatred. It was a pity the man could not think of anyone who would hate him so much. I turned to Creasy.

"Did you get the impression that any of the men hated Cody Jewett when you spoke to them? This was a crime of hatred, I'm certain of it."

"They seemed to like him well enough. According to their wives they were both men in bed and fast asleep when the attack happened. These fishermen work hard all day. When they return home they eat their suppers and go to bed. Now, Tom Tiley left you and came straight home that night, where I saw him. He and his sister are innocent, this we know."

Well, thought I, Margery might have a motive for hitting Cody Jewett over the head with a shovel, but she was too short for the blow that felled him. I lowered my head so that Creasy would not notice the flush I felt rising in my cheeks. He would not approve of my loose conduct and would lecture me and scold me—rightly so. Besides, he knew of my attachment to Alexandre Bernon. Not that I'd any mind to marry the Huguenot. I'd made a vow never to marry again after losing two beloved husbands. If Creasy learned of my tryst he would show me a long face and deliver a blistering sermon, perhaps even in public. I trusted Cody to remain silent about our afternoon, but gossip in a small village spread faster than a hawk diving at its prey. I was the stranger in Billingsgate—I would take the blame, not Cody. I was a Boston lady; what could you expect from a Boston lady? Of course I did provide employment for oyster gatherers and for the cask-makers so words would not be said to my face. My reputation would be torn to shreds behind my back. I did not care for that so much but word would hurt Margery and Tom, as well.

I changed the trend of my thoughts. "Look at the list I made, Creasy. Do you have any names to add? I've crossed off a few names, I think you'll agree with that."

He picked up the list, considering it with thin black brows drawn into an inverted letter V. He lifted his head, giving me a sharp look.

"Little Lucy Roach? You suspect little Lucy Roach of stabbing a man in the back and of felling a great ox like Cody Jewett?"

I was nettled by his tone of derision. Little Lucy Roach indeed! "Lucy Roach is a tall young woman. She is quite capable of lifting a shovel and smacking Cody Jewett over the head. She is much taller than her mother. You'll notice I crossed off Madame's name because of her short stature."

Creasy shook his head with enough vigor so that a lock of his hair escaped the black ribbon that held it back. The lock hung down the side of his face.

"Well, I'd rather suspect her father," I said. "I can't help it, I've taken a dislike to Robert Roach."

Creasy shook his head, the lock of hair flopping back and forth. "Jewett is in debt to Roach for nets and hooks and line. I took a look at the books. It doesn't make sense to try to kill a man who owes you money. Roach does not lack for sense, whatever you think of him. Cody Jewett pays off his debts on time, so long as he does that, Roach has no quarrel with him."

"Well, someone hates Cody. That same someone must have hated Charlie Pierce, too."

"Even though everyone claims to have liked Pierce, and everyone seems to respect Jewett." Creasy exhaled in a long breath. "I don't know, Hetty. Perhaps we should forget about this list for a time. Let's do something else. It may help to clear our minds, who knows? I have to go to Chequesett tomorrow and pray with Jack Warren's wife. I told him I would. If I don't speak to her I'm afraid Warren will take this other woman he fancies to wife. He'd become a bigamist, I told him, but he didn't seem to understand. They have their own ways here."

"Jack Warren's understanding doesn't exist," I said. "I'll come with you, if I may. I think you are right that we need to forget this business for awhile." I rose from the bed and set down the list upon my desk. It could wait until I had a clear head. It was time for dinner in any event, and I knew my cook would prepare something special for Creasy, who enjoyed a good dinner.

Sixteen

Next morning I commandeered a dory and rowed us across the bay. The day was perfect, the sun bright, the waters blue and the shores in the distance dressed in shrubs of red and gold. A brown duck bobbed in the water undisturbed by our passage. Gulls flew in the blue sky, their beaks silent of shrill cries. Creasy was unwontedly silent, a relief to me. No doubt the lovely day affected him with appreciation of its beauty, as it did me.

Chequesset Neck is a small point of land sticking out diagonally from the settlement of Billingsgate. The house of Mistress Fyte, Lucy's mother, was located by its lonesome, just beyond the beach where I pulled in. Creasy jumped out and pulled the boat up on to the sands.

We both heard the sounds of argument coming from the little house, gray and forlorn looking, some of its shingles missing, some hanging by a corner. We walked up to the door and Creasy pounded upon the silvered wood. I hoped he would not get a splinter in his hand. The door did not look too sturdy to me.

The voices stopped their loud argument. We waited for several minutes before the door opened a crack and two beady eyes peered out at us.

"Whaddayawan'?" The old woman's voice was belligerent.

Creasy cleared his throat and in his most sugary tones announced his name and that he was a minister from Boston. "I have been asked by Jack Warren to speak to his wife, Mary. Is she within?"

"Jusdaminit." The door slammed in Creasy's face.

I concealed the giggle that threatened to overcome me at the look of shock on my companion's face. He was not used to such treatment.

We could hear two voices arguing inside, then the door opened and two figures pushed their way out. The first was the owner of the beady eyes and suspicious voice, a short tubby figure dressed in sacking. The other was a much taller and younger woman—Mary Warren. Mary wore a man's stained shirt, a pair of trousers cut broad in the leg sailor-style and a pair of worn men's boots.

"Idonwanchainmahouseanymore," the mother said, speaking to her daughter. "Doncomback."

"Ma," Mary bleated, drawing out the word. She turned to Creasy and to me. "I ain't done nothin'." Her brown hair whipped across her plump face. Her lower lip thrust out. She did not meet our eyes.

"My good woman, I did not accuse you of anything," Creasy said, his tone soothing. He was very good with females from his training in the ministry. "I am come from your husband who very much wishes to reconcile with you."

"I ain't done nothin'," Mary repeated.

"You were married by a magistrate, three years ago, were you not?"

"We was legal married, he cannot say we was not." Mary clenched both her fists as if the point would be argued and she prepared to fight.

"Then why have you left the shelter of your husband's home?" Creasy asked this question in a tone that did not judge the woman but invited her to explain. After a few moments of silence Creasy prompted the woman. "Did he beat you?" Creasy asked this in a gentle voice.

Mary snorted. "Beat me? The little worm. I'd have hit him over the head with a skillet if he tried."

Mary's mother gave a snort of companionable agreement.

"Then why did you leave his house?" Creasy asked in genuine puzzlement.

Mary shifted her feet in their large boots. She hung her head. After several moments she answered the minister. "He don't take care of me like a man should."

"Oh. Does he neglect his husbandly duties?" Creasy asked the question but his face reddened.

Mary frowned. "He lets 'em make fun of us. He doesn't never tell 'em to stop. He let's 'em say things about me."

"I am told he has a bad back," Creasy said in a sort of apology. "No doubt he doesn't want to get into a fight."

"Who makes fun of you?" I interrupted Creasy's questioning. "Is it Cody Jewett? Does Cody make fun of you?" I looked Mary over. She had a large frame and strong, muscular arms.

Mary raised her head, glaring at me. "He better not. I guess I taught him better."

"And Charlie Pierce—did he make fun of you, too?"

Creasy began to object to my questioning but Mary pounced upon me before he could move. I found myself in an embrace of iron with a knife at my throat. She pushed me before her to the beach and to the dory waiting there. I was thrown bodily into the boat, landing upon my hands and knees and banging my head upon the prow. Before I could recover I felt the boat lurch and rock wildly while I held on to the seat with both hands. There was a splash of spray that soaked me, causing me to catch my breath as we were propelled forward. With powerful strokes the dory pulled away from shore. I managed to drag myself up to the seat and grab on to the sides of the boat, holding fast. I faced a murderous looking Mary with a knife held between her teeth and eyes glittering black as coal.

I heard cries behind me on the beach but I dared not turn. From the corner of my eye I saw by the angle that she was cutting across the bay towards the open waters. Mary rowed with swift, sure strokes and powerful oars. Would she dare the open waters of the Atlantic or would she turn bayside where there were coves and inlets and many places to hide? What would she do to me? I did not like the look of madness in those eyes but I did not dare move. She could drop the oars and be upon me with that knife. I decided to sit tight and be still. Conversation might upset her.

From the corner of my eye I could see the *Anhinga* tied to the Billingsgate docks and the sight restored some of my spirits. As soon as Creasy could get word to my crew, the *Anhinga* would be after us and not the great vast sweep of the ocean could hide us. My spirits raised even further when I spotted the boats setting off from the dock, bobbing like ducks upon the water. I prayed they were coming to intercept us. By her mad eyes, I was sure Mary did not yet see them. I must distract her from them as best I could. Conversation was the only means I had, even if it was to upset her. I would jump overboard if she made a move towards me; I had no other option. She would try to strike at me with the oars but I was a good swimmer.

"So you were the one who hit Cody Jewett with a shovel and tied him up for the tides to drown?"

Mary cackled. "An oar. I hit him with my oar blade. He went down like an ox." Mary lisped this with the knife in her mouth.

"That was a clever plan," I said. I hid my inward shudder. "He teased you, didn't he? Called you names?" Get her to talk, if she would, I thought. Keep her focus upon me.

She paused a moment to take the knife out of her mouth. She stuck it inside the shirt she wore, the handle convenient if she needed it.

"That Cody's a bad man. He called me an idiot and a bad name that sailors use for women. I don't like him. I tied him up so if he woke up in the water he wouldn't be able to swim to shore. Cody's a good swimmer."

"Can you swim?" I asked, curious.

She shook her head. "Can't swim. But I can row a dory as good as a man."

"Yes," I said, "you handle the oars very well."

"Thank you."

At least the woman had some manners! I kept on with my questions. "What about Charlie Pierce? Why did you kill him? Did he make fun of you?"

"No, not Charlie. He never made fun of me. But he wouldn't take me to the harvest festival." She pouted, her lower lip stuck out. "I asked him nice."

"Why would he refuse to take you?" I actually felt curious. What were this poor creature's mind processes?

"He said I had a husband to take me. Jack has a bad back. He couldn't take me, and so I told Charlie. I didn't mean that, you know. He paid me to take him across the bay. I didn't mean to kill him."

"What happened?" From the corner of my eye I saw the boats closing in.

"I asked him nice. He takes other ladies out, so I told him. He said as I wasn't a real lady and he only asked ladies who knew how to dress nice. And clean. He said I wasn't clean. Well, the other ladies don't fish for a living. He should have known that. What he didn't know was I stole his knife, the pretty knife he keeps for show. He don't clean fish with that knife. I wanted it. I wouldn't clean fish with it, either. Well, I asked him to change places with me and to row me for a change, because I said I had a blister on my hand, which I hadn't but I told him that. When he got up and turned his back I just up and stuck the knife in it. At first there was blood coming out but then he fell right over into the water. I just rowed away, that's all. I just rowed away. I didn't stay to see if he was drowned..."

I felt sick in my innards but I had to keep her talking.

"All because you don't have a dress?" I asked.

"I ain't got no fancy clothes. Charlie hadn't ought to laugh at me." Lucy's eyes glittered.

"No," I spoke as calmly as I could. "He shouldn't have laughed at you. Would you like a pretty dress? I can get you a pretty dress. What color would you like?" I was babbling at this point; anything to keep her focus. The dories were skimming across the water towards us.

"I saw a man had a red cloak once. It was a pretty color. I'd like to have a red dress with lots of white petticoats underneath." Mary gave me a wide smile. "But you won't give me one."

"Why not?"

"Because you'll be dead like Charlie."

"Oh?" I made an effort to shield the shivers that covered my arms from her eyes. "I can buy you a red dress with lots of white petticoats, but not if you kill me. Much better if you let me buy you that dress first, and then you can kill me." I hoped my reasoning would appeal to her.

"I don't know 'bout that," she said. "Besides, I ain't going to kill you. I can't kill anyone. The Bible says so. Besides, Charlie ain't dead. He walks abroad, my husband told me so. I didn't kill Cody Jewett. I could have smashed in his skull but I didn't. He was bleeding and the blood made me feel sick, so I tied him up and left him for the tides. The water should have killed him but he escaped. I'll bet Charlie let him loose. Them too were always thick. And I may have helped the water kill the minister's fat doxie, but that don't count. She was an injun. The water will kill you, too. I may have to hit you with the oar but the water will kill you, not me."

The minister's fat doxie? I knew the woman was mad, then. If Creasy had any doxie, fat or otherwise, I should have heard of it. I must try to argue her out of hurting me, since she evidently had some kind of scruples. "The water is my friend. It won't kill me." I raised my voice, for I could hear the clack of oars from the rescue boats. I did not dare turn my head to see how close they were. "How are you going to kill me if the water is my friend?"

Mary gave me a triumphant smile. She paused and leaned forward upon the oars. "I've got rope right here in this boat. You can't swim if you're all tied up, and there's no Charlie to rescue you. He don't even know you."

Shouts reached my ears. "Jump!" and "Dive Hetty, dive!"

I kicked off my shoes and dove over the prow. The water hit me with a shock but a blessed shock. I kicked beneath the surface, putting as much distance from that boat as I could before I breached.

When I surfaced a hand grabbed me by the neck of my smock and hauled me into the dory—a hairy hand, I noticed with gratitude. I gasped for breath and looked up into the concerned face of Sal, my first mate. I glanced over my shoulder.

Mary stood up in the boat, waving an oar about in the air.

"I'm going to broadside her!" Cody Jewett gave a loud shout, skimming his boat across the water.

His dory rammed into Mary's and the woman toppled over into the water. "I got her!" Cody shouted. He leaned over the side of his craft, reached down into the water and pulled up Mary Warren by her hair. He dragged her into the boat and we could see rope weaving back and forth as he secured her unresisting form.

"How did you know?" I gasped to Sal as I dragged myself upright on the seat.

"We saw a fire on the beach over at Chequesset. Jewett came looking for you and he said fire was a sign of trouble."

"That was Creasy," I said. "He saw Mary grab me but she had a knife at my throat so there was nothing he could do to stop her."

Cody Jewett looked up and yelled to me from his boat. "Hetty, are you unharmed?"

"Yes, I'm fine." I shouted back. "That's your murderer there. Can you get my shoes from Mary's boat?"

"Yes, I'm going to tow it back. Don't worry."

I sat there dripping water like a drowned rat, as happy as I could be. I cupped my hands for another yell. "I'm going to the ship to change my clothes. Will you take her to Roach's?"

Cody nodded his dark head with vigor.

"I'll see you there." I turned back in my seat to face Sal. "You'll send someone to pick up Creasy. The woman's mad, poor thing." Now that I was safe I could afford pity.

I thought I heard a mumble from Sal, something like, "Nine-lives of a cat."

SEVENTEEN

I thought it would be wise to set down in writing an account of Mary's confession to me and how it came about, so after I'd changed into dry clothing I penned a deposition which I signed. I had Sal witness it. This paper I brought with me. I had no sooner set foot upon the dock than I was greeted by Tom Tiley and his sister.

Margery embraced me in a fierce hug. "Oh, Hetty! You might have been killed! Why didn't you come to us? I've wanted to thank you a thousand times for saving Cody's life."

Tom stood back, a shy smile on his face. "I want to thank you for finding Charlie's killer. Mary confessed to it."

"Yes, I want to thank you for that, too," Margery said. She released me. "Now that this horrid business is over, Cody and I can marry."

Was there a warning look in her eyes or was my guilt placing it there? I managed to keep my composure. "You must let me know the date and I shall send a wedding present. I'm on my way over to Mister Roach's house where they brought Mary. I wrote out an account of what happened to me." I showed them the paper in my hand. "I'll be leaving in the morning." Did I see a look of relief in Margery's eyes?

"We'll walk with you," Tom said.

Margery took my arm, talking about how brave I was and how glad were they that Mister Cotton Mather had sent me to them. I thought rather her hands should be around my throat throttling me. It was all Alexandre Bernon's fault for sailing to England on me. Well, most of it was, I amended. When we reached Roach's residence I pulled back, alarmed by the crowd waiting outside his door. It looked as if the whole village was there—perhaps the whole population of Cape Cod! There were certainly murmurs and whispers as we pushed our way through and Tom knocked heavily upon the door.

Madame Roach answered, opening the door a crack and peering through. "Oh, it's you," she said, squinting at me. "I suppose you had best come inside." She gestured us through, as the while grumbling. "I don't know why everybody is coming to my house. It's not as if Mister Roach is the constable, for he's not. We've had to lock up the prisoner in our shed and now everyone had come hoping for a peep at her, except there's no window in the shed and right glad am I for that else we would be swamped with callers."

"I have brought a deposition with me which I hope your husband will keep in his care." I waved the sealed paper at her. "I leave tomorrow morning on the tide."

I squeezed past the woman, dragging Margery with me. Tom followed.

"Well, come in then," Madame said in grudging tones, following us.

Robert Roach sat upon a stool before the hearth. Next to him on another stool sat Cody Jewett. Cody rose as we entered, his grin for me or for Margery I could not tell. I ignored him and handed my paper to Roach.

"I wrote out a deposition—my account of what happened when Mary captured me, and of her confession to me. I hope you will accept it and keep it until such time as the constable arrives or whatever officials hear the case. I must return to Boston tomorrow on the tide."

Roach accepted the paper, small brown teeth showing in a smile. "I hear you had quite an adventure with our Mary."

Adventure, thought I? Our Mary? As if she were a naughty schoolgirl? Let him face a murderous madwoman with a knife in her mouth. I hoped he would some day.

Cody held out a sack to me. "Your shoes," he said.

I took the sack but noticed his eyes went past me to Margery. He smiled at her. I felt a slight pang; it was obvious how fond he was of the woman. I'd known it from the start yet there was a part of me that did indeed belong to Cody. Best to forget that, I thought. It had been my own fault, that coupling, with no thought for Margery. Any pangs on my part were my penance.

"Cody insists upon staying with us to guard the prisoner." Roach made a small bow in Cody's direction. "I say she is safe enough. The only one we allowed to see her is her husband, and that only for a few moments."

"There are people outside who would tear her limb from limb if they got hold of her," Cody said in a growl.

Our heads turned at a loud knock upon the door.

"Mercy, who can this be? As if we are not crowded enough in our own home with all these people," Madame grumbled but she went to the door quick enough.

Creasy entered the room, giving Madame a gallant bow and a short bow for the two men. Me, he ignored.

"I've just come from prayers with Jack Warren. He begged me to pray with his wife. I hope you will allow me to bring to her the comfort of the gospel?" He looked to Robert Roach. "Even those who sin deserve an opportunity to repent of their sins," he said.

Roach merely nodded. Madame Roach clasped her hands together with an exclamation. "Oh, how kind of you, sir!"

"What, comfort for a murderer?" Cody frowned, black brows drawn like a thundercloud. "She don't deserve any comfort, not that one. She would've killed Hetty, too, you know."

"Indeed," Creasy drew himself straight, "I was afraid she would. I must thank you, Mister Jewett, for your timely intervention."

I felt indignant but Cody spoke before I could. "She saved herself, you know. Hetty is a resourceful woman. I only captured Mary."

"No one knows that Hetty is resourceful better than I."

The two men bristled at each other like two dogs over a bone.

I did not wish to be the bone. I addressed Creasy. "I'm sure it's your duty to pray for that woman's repentance and redemption and I wish you success, but I must return to my ship. We sail at dawn if you sail with us, Mister Cotton."

Creasy made a bow to the company in general and took his leave. Madame followed him, saying that she would show him the way.

Roach waved my deposition at me. "May I read this before you go?"

I nodded and took a seat upon a table bench. I watched as Cody took Margery by the hand, settling her upon the stool he had just vacated. Tom Tiley stood in the middle of the room.

A loud scream brought us to our feet. Tiley bolted out the door, the rest of us at his heels. I shoved past Robert Roach, Cody Jewett shoved past me. He barked at us to stay back. Margery hesitated behind Roach. We followed Tom around the side of the house. With one mind we all stopped short. Before us Creasy Cotton stood cradling Madame Roach in his arms, and she sobbing upon his waistcoat. Cody held up a hand to halt us. He moved like a panther to the open door of the shed, took a quick look and once more held up his hand. We were rooted like statues.

"She's dead. She hung herself."

There was a collective sigh; I drew in my breath and forced myself to swallow.

Cody shook his head. "It's not a pretty sight. Roach, you take the women inside. Tom, come help me cut her down."

I thought perhaps I should see for myself but was just as glad—relieved, really—when Robert Roach touched my shoulder and herded me with the other women including his wife, inside the house. Creasy and poor Madame had seen it for me. Roach led his wife to one of the stools and seated her upon it. His face was as white as hers. Creasy seated himself beside me upon the bench and Margery occupied the second stool. Her face was as blank as I felt mine must be.

Within five minutes Cody and Tom reentered the house.

Cody's dark eyes were hooded, his expression serious.

"What can I do to help?" Creasy was the first one to speak.

I answered then, addressing Creasy. "Perhaps you should be the one to tell Jack Warren. Someone must do it."

Creasy looked at Cody Jewett and moved at his nod.

"Tom, go get Annie." Cody's direction was brief.

"I'll help Annie lay her out." Margery's voice was steady.

I looked over at Madame and addressed myself to Robert Roach. "Sir, your wife has had a shock. You should give her a sip of brandy and put her to bed. In fact, we could all use a sip. Don't worry, I'll pay for it," I added as his anxious brows rose.

Roach dug through his stock and came up with a small cask and a mug. He gave his wife the first sip and himself took the second, before passing it to the rest of us. I took a large sip. The warmth from the golden liquid spread through my limbs. I hadn't realized how cold and tired I'd felt. And sad. If only people had been kind to Mary perhaps all this might have been avoided. I walked up to Cody. "Do you need me for anything?"

Cody reached out and took my hand, giving it a squeeze. "I'll always need you, darling girl." He raised my hand to his lips like a practiced cavalier. "But I'm shortly to be a married man."

I'm certain my look was sour. I was in no mood for frolics. I walked out the door.

Creasy came on board early the next morning as we prepared to set sail. With him were Tom Tiley and his sister. I found I could meet Margery's eyes with tolerable composure.

"We've come to thank you for everything you've done for us, Hetty. Now we can sleep safely in our beds." Margery handed me a heavy sack. "It's not much, only some apples we picked for you."

"Come see us again, Hetty. I hope it will be a happier time." Tom shifted his feet.

A good night's sleep had restored my frame of mind. I gave Margery a quick hug. "Next time we meet you'll be a married lady. Let me know when the date is to be and I will send you the best present I can find." I discovered that I did wish her happiness in her married life. Marriage to Cody Jewett would be a challenge.

The brother and sister were small waving figures once we'd set sail for Boston. The thought of that bustling city did wonders to raise my spirits. I left Creasy at the rail to watch as the shoreline of the Cape receded. He had a contemplative look upon his face; he fingered something strung around his neck. It was Creasy's fate to moon over the wrong women, I thought. As for me, I had no time for sentiment. Commercial matters awaited my attention. I'd neglected my own business interests far too long, but then justice had been served on Cape Cod and my late husband, Mr. Henry the magistrate, taught me that justice must ever take priority for any good citizen of the community. I had done my duty to the Bay Colony and to its most famous denizen, minister Cotton Mather.

Postscript: I did my best to track down the late Mister Pierce's fiancée using all my contacts but could find no woman engaged to that gentleman. One of my contacts did find a bawdy house where Charlie Pierce was well known and much grieved. "A liberal gentleman," as one young lady described him, holding a scrap of linen to her moist eyes.

photo by
Megan Mumford

About Author M.E. Kemp

M. E. Kemp was born in Oxford, MA, a town her ancestors settled in 1713. With her Grandmother's tales of family adventures and her father's interest in American history, Kemp became an avid fan of New England's colonial history, writing a prize-winning short story in middle school and continuing with articles that appeared in national magazines. She writes a current series of historical mystery novels featuring two nosy Puritans as detectives. She is married to Jack H. Rothstein and lives in Saratoga Springs, site of many of her short stories concerning the Revolutionary War Battle of Saratoga. Her two kitties, Boris and Natasha, often reenact that battle for her.

Check out Kemp's work at: www.mekempmysteries.com

Another great read by M.E. Kemp

Death of a Dancing Master

Print ISBN 978-1-60318-240-9
Ebook ISBN 978-1-60318-241-6

It's 1693, and Boston's dancing master is found dead with a fencing foil through his gut.

Two nosy Puritans, Hetty Henry and Creasy Cotton, are asked to investigate. The young minister who found the body has been arrested for the murder but Hetty and Creasy discover there are many other suspects including the town's ministers who preached forcefully against him, the magistrates who harassed him with fines, angry husbands, and jealous women who contended for his affections. Hetty interviews the ladies who willingly confess their love for the dancing master—several confess to causing his death. Unfortunately, none of the ladies know the real means of his murder.

Creasy has no luck when questioning the men, either. Later, a tavern wench gives him a note asking for a meeting, claiming she has information about the murder. When Creasy turns up for their midnight meeting he gets an unpleasant surprise. Hetty devises a plan is to set up a trap using herself as bait. She claims to know the killer's secret and demands payment for her silence. The cemetery meeting at midnight becomes a fight for Hetty's life…

CPSIA information can be obtained at www.ICGtesting.com
Printed in the USA
BVOW021620041112

304442BV00004B/1/P

9 781603 184786